Bird In Flight . . .

"You can't fly down here every single weekend!"

"I can and I will."

"We'll only make each other miserable. It won't last, Kyle. One of us will be hurt in the end."

He sighed in exasperation. "Damn it, you've been fighting me at every turn from the moment we met. Why? Didn't this weekend mean anything to you? Can't you even give an inch? Don't you care enough to make this work?"

"Yes, I care about you!" she cried. "More than any man I've ever met. And I'll be miserable the moment you leave. But a long-distance relationship can't work. It's impossible."

"How do you know it's impossible?" he asked fiercely. "Have you ever tried it?"

"Yes."

"When?"

"When I left my husband!"

Dear Reader,

Welcome to Silhouette! Our goal is to give you hours of unbeatable reading pleasure, and we hope you'll enjoy each month's six new Silhouette Desires. These sensual, provocative love stories are both believable and compelling—sometimes they're poignant, sometimes humorous, but always enjoyable.

Indulge yourself. Experience all the passion and excitement of falling in love along with our heroine as she meets the irresistible man of her dreams and together they overcome all obstacles in the path to a happy ending.

If this is your first Desire, I hope it'll be the first of many. If you're already a Silhouette Desire reader, thanks for your support! Look for some of your favorite authors in the coming months: Stephanie James, Diana Palmer, Dixie Browning, Ann Major and Doreen Owens Malek, to name just a few.

Happy reading!

Isabel Swift
Senior Editor

SDRL-7/85

SYRIE A. ASTRAHAN
Songbird

 Silhouette Desire

Published by Silhouette Books New York

America's Publisher of Contemporary Romance

SILHOUETTE BOOKS
300 E. 42nd St., New York, N.Y. 10017

ISBN: 0-373-05262-6

First Silhouette Books printing February 1986

SYRIE A. ASTRAHAN

wrote her first book when she was in sixth grade, and hasn't stopped writing since. She has worked in journalism, television, theater and advertising design, and especially enjoys writing romances about whirlwind courtships. It's easy to see why: she and her husband, Bill, met in college, fell in love and became engaged three weeks later! "Love, laughter, a worthy goal and an enjoyable occupation are the keys to a happy life," says Syrie, who resides in California. She likes to read, travel, eat strawberry short-cake, receive letters from her readers and invent stories for her two young sons, Ryan and Jeffrey.

This book is dedicated with deep affection
and gratitude . . .

to Grandpa Joe, who brought joy and laughter to the lives
of all who knew him

to Nannie, whose sunny disposition will be an inspiration
to me always

to my parents, for their faith and encouragement

and to Bill, for love that knows no bounds

One

___

The song ended. Desiree leaned forward on the high stool, bringing her lips close to the padded microphone. "That was Rita Coolidge singing the hit from her new album, 'Be Mine Tonight.' Before that we heard from Johnny Mathis with 'So in Love with You.'"

She checked the pie-sized clock on the wall above the console. "It's twenty-five past three here on this hot and sunny Wednesday afternoon in June. You're listening to KICK Anaheim, 102 on your FM dial. This is Desiree keeping you company for that long drive home."

Right on cue, the first soft notes of the next song began to play. Desiree removed the massive gray headphones and lifted her toffee-colored curls off her shoulders, letting the cool air from the overhead vent flow freely around her neck. A fire-engine red bumper sticker affixed to the window above the console caught her eye: SPEND THE NIGHT WITH DESIREE...KICK 102 FM!

Time for a new slogan, she thought, carefully peeling the length of vinyl off the glass and tossing it in the trash. Seven years of working evenings and nights, and you finally made it: Prime time, daytime radio in Southern California! So whatever you do, she thought, don't blow it.

She turned up the volume control, leaned her head back and closed her eyes, hoping the mellow tune's soothing rhythm would numb her senses. It's the same job as before, she told herself, only the time has changed. Forget about Arbitron and shares and rating points. Forget about the hundreds of would-be deejays standing in the wings, chomping at the bit, just waiting for you to mess up. Put it out of your mind! You're good—one of the best jocks this station has—or Sam wouldn't have given you the afternoon drive. Just relax and enjoy yourself.

She heard the studio door open and straightened up, blinking open her amber eyes. Tom, the station's part-time gofer, rushed in, his forehead perspiring beneath a tangle of wiry red hair.

"Man, it's hot out there," he said, fanning his youthful face with a stack of small newsprint sheets. "You're lucky they air-condition this cubicle of yours."

"Cubicle is right." Desiree glanced about the tiny studio, where dog-eared posters of Elvis, The Beatles, Kenny Rogers and Streisand were plastered across the dingy beige walls. "There are people who get claustrophobic in elevators. How do I stand it in here for four straight hours without climbing the walls?"

Tom grinned. "You love it, beautiful, and you know it." He handed her the stack of newsprint.

"Anything good?"

"Are you kidding? What do you think this is, *Sixty Minutes*?"

She leafed through the pile of news briefs, fresh off the wire. "'New smoking control law giving people nicotine fits,'" she read aloud. "Cute, but no cigar. Here's another prize. 'Millionaire Owner of Laundromat chain taken to the cleaners in palimony suit.'" She shook her head, smiling. "Give me a break! Why do we bother with this stuff? We're not a news station."

"Don't ask me." Tom shrugged as he turned to leave. "Sam likes this junk. And one must never argue with the P.D." Before shutting the door, he scrunched up his face and mimicked their program director's gravelly voice. "Just remember my motto—Be Entertaining."

Desiree laughed as she slipped on her headphones. "I'll give it my best shot. Today's news can use all the help it can get."

A familiar refrain signaled the end of the song. She pushed the start button on the deck to the left of the console. A glance at the digital countdown timer told her she had fifteen seconds. Just then Tom pressed his face up against the glass of the window above the console, staring in at her with distorted fleshy lips and huge bug-eyes.

She smothered a laugh. "If you're sitting in traffic out there right now, feeling that tension just creeping up your spine, I've got the perfect way to get rid of all that stress. Tell yourself Desiree's sitting right next to you in the front seat, giving you a nice long intimate massage." As soon as she said the words, she cringed inwardly. Intimate massage? Good grief! Did I really say that?

The commercial break began. She again plucked off her headphones and glanced up at Tom, who was rolling his eyes as he walked away, mouthing the word "outrageous" at her through the glass.

Outrageous. That's what the reporter from the Los Angeles Times had written about her in this morning's review of her new afternoon show. "One outrageous, sexy woman...whose luscious lusty voice could, with one well-placed sigh, bring half the male population of Southern California to its knees."

She laughed softly to herself. Luscious? Lusty? Hardly. She believed she was reasonably attractive. Steve, her ex-husband, had once told her she had eyes like molten gold and a face like a cameo—small and oval, with a thin straight nose and a flawless creamy complexion. Her hair seemed to match her personality. It brushed her shoulders in thick unruly waves, a blend of vibrant shades from light brown to red to rich dark maple. But somehow, her deep voice led people to expect a tall voluptuous blond bombshell who walked, talked and breathed sex. No way on earth could she ever hope to fit that image.

She was petite in every sense of the word. She possessed a few small curves in all the right places, but no matter how hard she tried she didn't quite reach the five-foot-one-inch mark. Thirty years old, she had endured a lifetime of jokes about the discrepancy between her voice and her looks. She'd seen the disappointment in people's eyes too many times when they met her and discovered she wasn't the sex symbol they'd imagined.

Still, her voice was her biggest asset. Sam insisted that teasing banter meant higher ratings. The listeners couldn't see her, after all. What harm could there be in playing along?

She scanned the news brief she'd selected, waiting for the commercial break to end, then threw the mike switch to program and turned up the volume.

"Here's an item of interest for all you soda-pop guzzlers out there. Looks like the new diet soft drink, Sparkle Light, is losing steam. In an unexpected move yesterday, the parent corporation, privately owned, multimillion dollar Harrison Industries, announced plans for Sparkle Light Bottling Company to go public." She went on to read the experts' analysis, which pointed a finger at a suspected drop in product sales, then laid the news bulletin up on the counter.

"If you've always wanted to own stock in a soft-drink company, this might be your big chance. But let's hope Sparkle Light picks up in a hurry, or you may find yourself making a big deposit, no-return investment on a warehouse full of pop without any fizz!"

She played a groaning sound-effects tape. Next, grabbing a large pink index card from the board above her console, she announced it was time to play the Trivia Game. "I hope you're all next to your phones. The number to call is 555-KICK. I'll take caller number twelve."

All five lines on the multitap phone in her studio lit up with magical precision. Desiree smiled. The immediate response to contests on the afternoon drive never ceased to amaze her. This was the time of day to be on the air!

"The caller who can answer today's trivia question correctly will receive a complimentary dinner for two at Maximillian's in Huntington Beach." She read a blurb about the restaurant, then punched the buttons on the phone one at a time, counting out loud and disconnecting each line in sequence.

"Hi! You're on the air," she said when she reached the twelfth caller. "Who's this?"

"This is Kyle Harrison." The voice, obscured slightly by faint background noise, sounded low, smooth and deeply masculine. She found herself sitting up straight on the stool, listening attentively.

"Hello, Kyle." She conjured up a quick mental image to fit the voice. Tan...athletically built...about thirty-five and devilishly handsome? No. People never look the way they sound. And you, Desiree, ought to know that better than anyone. Odds are he's short, fat and fiftyish with beady eyes and a huge nose. "Did you know you've got a terrific radio voice, Kyle?"

"Thanks. Yours isn't bad either." He sounded irritated. "Listen, I'm calling—"

"Are you as good-looking as you sound?" she teased.

A split-second pause. Then, he replied curtly, "Depends on your point of view. Are you?"

Oh, God. Open mouth, insert foot. She glanced down at her worn, tight-fitting cutoffs and clinging pink T-shirt. What kind of woman was he imagining? A gorgeous blonde in a sexy magazine cover shot? Think fast. Be Entertaining.

"Just let your imagination go wild," she said in her most velvety voice. "If only you could see the wicked little dress I've got on today. Electric-blue silk. Open in the back. Cut just off the shoulder. Terribly chic. And these silver spiked heels are positively sinful."

"I'll bet." He laughed suddenly, a deep pleasant laugh which set her spine tingling.

What a gorgeous laugh, she thought. Maybe he isn't quite so old or so ugly after all. Get to the trivia question, an inner voice warned. You've talked to him too long already. But instead she leaned forward on the console, resting her chin on her hand. "Where are you from, Kyle?"

"Seattle."

"Seattle! That's a thousand miles away. KICK's coverage must be even more widespread than I thought."

He laughed again. "Sorry to disappoint you. I'm only about thirty miles away, near the L.A. airport. At this moment I'm crawling along on the San Diego freeway, bumper-to-bumper, at the incredible speed of three miles per hour."

"A car-phone executive!" she announced with delight. "My very first one on the air. You just made my day."

"Briefcase phone, actually. It's a rented car."

"Oh!" Mobile phones cost thousands of dollars. A new, even less flattering image of the man formed in her mind: a cigar-smoking corporate executive in a dark blue suit, three enormous diamond rings flashing on each stubby hand. Age: sixty. Eyes: watery-gray. Hair: none. "Well, Kyle, I hope you can think trivia and drive at the same time, because—"

"Hold on," he interrupted. "I know this is a contest line, but I called for another reason—to comment on a news item you gave about a company of mine a few minutes back. Sparkle Light."

She opened her mouth to reply, then froze. Sparkle Light! In a flash of belated understanding she realized the significance of his name. Kyle Harrison. Harrison Industries! The privately-owned parent corporation. Desperately she began to riffle through the stack of newsprint on her counter, her mind racing, trying to remember what she'd said about Sparkle Light. Something about a no-return investment, the product losing its fizz... Had she sounded overly sarcastic? Defamatory? If only we had a seven-second delay system, she thought, so I could bleep out his comments if he starts to get nasty.

"The information you gave was essentially correct. Sparkle Light is going public. But the so-called expert analysis you read was completely off base. Since you popped up with your phone number so conveniently I thought I'd call and set the record straight."

"Well, thank you, Mr. Harrison," she said, hoping her voice sounded as light and sparkling as his product. "We always welcome a little inside information from the business world." Why did she suddenly feel as if she had to call him mister? From now on I'm going to start screening calls, she thought. To hell with spontaneity!

"We're going public to raise capital for other investments. It's that simple. The move is no reflection on the sales record of Sparkle Light. In fact the product has far exceeded our sales projections, and—"

"That's wonderful, Mr. Harrison," she cut in quickly. "And I apologize if I gave out any information that was incorrect or misleading. Our news comes straight from UPI in New York, and we can't verify every—"

"I understand that. But your commentary doesn't come from New York."

Her stomach tightened into a knot. Sam would kill her for this. Absolutely kill her. "I'm so glad you called to straighten me out, Mr. Harrison." She cued up the next song, struggling to keep her voice calm. "We—"

"I'm ready for that trivia question now."

"Wh-what?"

"This is supposed to be a trivia contest, isn't it? Something about a free dinner for two?"

"Oh! Yes!" Her fingers trembled as she reached for a small box with the words THE TRIVIA GAME emblazoned across the lid. He really got a kick out of putting her on the spot, didn't he? Well, she'd give the creep a hard one. She took a deep breath to steady herself and pulled a bright yellow and green game card from the box. "Today's category is science. Are you ready?"

"Ready."

This'll get him, she thought. "What country built the first successful helicopter, and in what year?"

Without a moment's hesitation, he said, "Germany. The FW-61. In 1936."

Desiree's mouth dropped open. How did he know that? The damn obnoxious man had to be a trivia king on top of everything else. "That's correct! You're our winner for today." Trying to sound enthusiastic, she added, "Congratulations. If you'll stay on the line, I'll have someone explain where you can pick up your prize." She punched the hold button on the phone. Play the next song, she instructed herself, going through the motions mechanically. And for God's sake, don't try to say anything cute. "Okay! Coming up, three great tunes in a row from KICK 102 FM, your mellow music station."

Blowing out a relieved breath, Desiree punched another phone line and called the receptionist in the front office. "Barbara? The contest winner's on line one. Would you take care of him, please?" She hung up without waiting for a reply. The radio broadcast was piped throughout the building; she could count on Barbara to assess the situation.

Just then the studio door burst open. It was Sam.

"Since when did you become a stockbroker?" he bellowed, eyes blazing in a tanned face surrounded by thinning dark hair. "No one asked for your advice. We play music around here, not the stock market!"

"I know. I just—"

"Stick to sports and the weather from now on. Leave Wall Street to the experts. Got it?" The door slammed.

Terrific, she thought.

The door opened again. "And another thing!" Sam yelled. "Don't chitchat with people on the air. We're a music station. If you want to do talk radio, go get a job at KTLK!"

She sighed deeply as the door slammed once more. She should never have commented on the news release. And she certainly shouldn't have talked so long on the air with Kyle Harrison! Whatever had possessed her? She was luckly Sam hadn't fired her. One false move and a deejay was usually out the door. It's going to take a lot more than one rave newspaper review to keep me on the afternoon drive now, she thought with a frown.

Dejectedly, she studied the rotation chart taped to the window above the console. A hit tune—or type "A" song—was next. Reaching aside to the revolving music rack, she pulled the next cartridge in sequence from the row marked "A" and slipped it into the deck. It was a new Anne Murray hit—a real heartbreaker, and one of her favorites.

Suddenly the lyrics of the song on the air caught her attention. The tone was tender, with an underlying melancholy.

Desiree's eyes crinkled with a familiar pang of sadness. She felt an affinity with the singer, as if the words about long and lonely nights were being sung solely to her, about her. But that's ridiculous, she thought. Her career demanded that she be self-sufficient and totally independent, and over the past five years she'd come to like it that way. So why was she partial to these tear-jerking love songs? Why did they always bring a lump to her throat?

She grabbed a pencil and scratch pad to jot down the titles of the songs coming up, so she could list them later on the air. But for some reason her pencil stood poised and motionless as a smooth deeply masculine voice drifted into her consciousness. A voice that set her spine tingling, a voice a prince would be proud of. She shook her head. Too bad he turned out to be such a toad.

Several minutes later a tall buxom brunette in a gaily striped sundress hurried into the studio, waving a candy bar. "Time for a junk-food break. I know you like peanut butter cups but the machine was out." Her nose was slightly crooked, her accent unmistakably Brooklyn. "Hey, what's the frown for? Did Sam read you the riot act?"

Desiree shrugged as she slid off her stool, grabbed the candy bar and tore off its wrapper. "Yeah. But apparently I'm still employed. For today, anyway." She took a bite of the candy bar. "Mmmm. Hits the spot. Thanks, Barb. I've been eating celery all week. Another piece and I'd probably turn green."

Barbara pursed her lips in mock irritation. "As if you need to watch what you eat, you skinny thing."

"I do. Constantly. It's a cross all short people must bear. You Amazons don't know how lucky you are."

Barbara laughed and handed her a phone message. "Listen, I just got a call from a lady at Barney's, a new restaurant in Orange. They want to know if you'll host their opening-night party next month."

As she stared at the note, Desiree felt a stab of disappointment like a knife between the ribs. She couldn't do it, of course. It was impossible. She sighed. "You gave her the usual polite refusal, I hope?"

Barbara shook her head. "No, I didn't. I told her you'd think about it."

"Think about it? What's there to think about?" She handed back the note. "I can't do it. You know that."

"I don't know anything of the kind. You've got to stop hiding from your fans, Des. The lady raved about your voice! It'd be great publicity for you."

"Some great publicity. They're expecting a glamorous Candice Bergen-type and instead they get Shirley Temple."

"Would you come off it? You might be short, but with your hair up, in the right kind of dress, you'd look glamorous as hell." She gestured emphatically with both hands. "And besides, you're gorgeous! I'd give a million bucks for a face like yours."

"For this face?" Desiree thrust out her front teeth and wiggled her jaw in chipmunk fashion. "Well, I'd give a million bucks to be about seven inches taller, have your tan and wear your bra size."

Barbara laughed. "God, Desiree, you're so dense. Plenty of men go gaga over petite women. You don't know a good thing when you've got it."

"I don't want men to go gaga over me. I'm perfectly happy the way I am."

"The hell you are. No one could be happy living the way you do, except possibly a nun. When's the last time you went out on a date? Invited a man over to your house? Two years ago? Three?"

"Barb, I've told you before, I'm not about to get involved with anyone again. You know what happened to my one attempt at marriage. And look at Dave. Look at Mike, and John. Divorced, every one of them." She finished the last bite of the candy bar and sighed. "Believe me, relationships and radio don't mix."

"Who's talking about relationships? I'm talking date here. A simple night out with a guy." Barbara shook her head in disgust. "Just because that husband of yours was a louse doesn't mean you should swear off men for the rest of your life. The other jocks sure haven't sworn off women."

Steve wasn't a louse, Desiree thought. But there was no sense arguing with Barbara about it. She glanced back at the digital countdown timer on the console. "Listen, I hate to eat and run, Barb, but I'm on in thirty seconds."

"Okay. Bye." Barbara backed up and paused in the doorway. "By the way, no matter what Sam said, I think you handled the guy on the phone like a pro."

"Thanks a bunch."

"No, I mean it. He pulled a dirty trick, calling on the contest line and springing all that stuff on you over the air. When he comes in to pick up his free dinner pass tonight, I promise I'll be as nasty as possible."

Desiree grinned as Barbara pulled the door shut. "Do that."

Five-thirty. Desiree began to hum to herself. A half hour more and I'm out the door, she thought. And I know exactly what I'm going to do when I get home. Take my phone off the hook and curl up in bed with a glass of wine and a good book.

She waited for her cue, then said into the mike, "That was 'Songbird,' by Barbra Streisand. It's always been a special favorite of mine."

Behind her, she heard the studio door open quietly and thought, Barbara again? Didn't she see the red warning light? She knows better than to come in while I'm on the air.

"I hope you're taking advantage of the beautiful weather we're having this evening. The summer equinox is next week, the longest day of the year." The door clicked shut softly behind her. "So go out and enjoy all those extra hours of daylight. Take a walk on the beach with your loved one and think of me." She took off her headphones as the commercial break began. Three more tunes, she thought. Then the traffic report.

"You do that well."

The voice from behind startled her so much she jumped up from her stool. Instinctively she knew who it was; there was no mistaking the deep resonant Radio Voice. But what was he doing back here?

She whirled around and froze, clutching her headphones. Surprise rendered her speechless. This was Kyle Harrison?

TWO

Where was the fat balding business executive she'd envisioned, the man who smoked cigars and wore half a dozen diamond rings? Desiree had been certain Kyle Harrison would look exactly the opposite of the way he sounded. But even in her wildest dreams, her most outlandish fantasies, she could never have imagined anyone so handsome. This man was—quite simply—devastating.

He stood with his back against the closed door of the studio, his arms crossed over his broad chest, studying her through dark-green eyes twinkling with what seemed like mingled curiosity and amusement. He must be in his mid-thirties, she decided, incredibly young to be sole owner of a multimillion-dollar corporation like Harrison Industries.

At first he seemed tall, at least six feet. But then, judging the difference in their heights to be closer to nine inches, she attributed his apparent tallness to the way his chest tapered to a narrow waist and hips, or to the slim fit of his camel-brown slacks over long well-proportioned legs. The short sleeves of his white dress shirt exposed tanned muscular forearms. His conservatively cut, rusty-brown hair fell in thick natural waves. An upturned nose reigned over perfectly formed lips, which at this moment, were twitching slightly, as if he was enjoying some private joke at her expense.

"I'm glad to see there really is a beautiful woman behind the beautiful voice."

She saw a curiously stunned look in his dancing green eyes as they traveled the length of her slender figure, from her shapely bare legs to her tight-fitting cutoffs and T-shirt. "I was afraid I was going to find an old man operating some sort of electronic synthesizer, like in *The Wizard of Oz*."

Desiree felt herself blushing under his scrutiny. Funny she'd expected him to be an old man, too.

"Thanks for letting me come back here. I wasn't sure if you would, after what I said on the air a while ago. I wanted to apologize for getting you in trouble. Your receptionist told me what happened."

She tried to speak, but her tongue had uncooperatively glued itself to the roof of her mouth. Say something, you idiot, she screamed silently. Tell him you *didn't* let him come back here! Tell him it was Barbara's idea! Tell him to get out! Instead she found her eyes drawn to the riot of curly brown hair peeking out above the open neck of his shirt. A tie should be there, she thought. A monogrammed silk tie.

"I know you talk. I just heard you." His green eyes seemed to search her face for an explanation of her silence.

A sudden gust of air from the air conditioner buffeted her hair and sent goose bumps racing madly up her arms and neck. To her dismay she felt her nipples harden beneath her thin bra and T-shirt from the sudden chill, and she looked away, her heart pounding.

Then, furious with herself for looking away, she glared back at him. What had he called her before? A beautiful woman? Hah! He's just being polite, to mask his disappointment on seeing the real me. If he said one word about the electric-blue silk dress and the silver spiked heels, she'd kill him.

But he didn't. He took a step forward, smiling warmly, his eyes riveted to her face. He leaned one elbow on the high counter running the length of the small room.

"I understand your boss had a minor coronary after my call, and threatened to transfer you to Siberia."

She felt a smile start and fought to tighten her lips into a firm straight line. I'm angry with this man, she reminded herself. He embarrassed me on the air and caused my employer to scream at me. I will not let him charm me. I will not smile.

"But I understand there are a few radio stations in Siberia, so you should be all right. If they're enlightened enough to hire female deejays in Russia."

A giggle bubbled up in her chest. Then, against her will, a long deep laugh escaped her control. She shot him a wary glance, then spoke with a deadpan face. "I don't think I'd do too well at the job. I don't speak Russian."

"Ah!" He laughed. "A point I hadn't considered."

She studied him for a moment, biting her lip to keep from grinning. When he laughed, his eyes crinkled and he threw his head back, chuckling from deep down in his chest. It was a nice laugh. She noticed his glance travel downward and stop in the vicinity of her chest, where her taut nipples now visibly strained against her thin pink cotton shirt.

"I—I haven't interrupted anything important, have I?" His voice seemed to have risen a note or two. He cleared his throat. "Do you have to go on the air?"

Oh God, she thought, whirling back to the console with a sudden rush of panic. I forgot all about— To her horror, the commercial break was nearly over. Another three seconds and she'd have had dead air. She was in enough trouble already without that. Quickly she turned up the volume in the studio and made a smooth transition into the next tune.

"That was a close call." She sighed with relief. Lowering the volume again, she pulled out two cartridges from the music rack, nearly dropping them in the process. What was wrong with her, she wondered as she set up the next two songs. She'd been working in the studio five days a week for nearly two years. Why was she suddenly all thumbs?

"I'm sorry if I'm distracting you. I suppose I shouldn't be in here."

She looked back at him. He still leaned against the counter, gazing at her with a compelling warmth. No, you shouldn't, she thought. "It's all right," she said. "I don't have to talk for a while."

"That's too bad." His voice was deep and soft. "I like listening."

A strange inexplicable heat coursed through her body and she backed up into the stool, almost knocking it over. She couldn't believe this was happening to her. She'd never reacted so strongly to any man before, not even when she first met Steve.

Apparently he misinterpreted the cause of her confusion. His brow furrowed and his eyes filled with sudden concern. "Hey, if you're worried about your job, don't be. I just spoke with your manager, and I think you're off the hook."

"Off the hook? What do you mean?"

"I mean, I just bought a sizeable advertising package for Sparkle Light. Blankets the next three weeks and continues well into next year. With strict instructions that our spots run only during your show."

She stared at him, at first not quite comprehending what he'd just said. Then, as the impact of his words filtered into her brain, she swallowed, ran her tongue lightly over her lips and said, "That ought to make Sam dance in the aisles." And it certainly won't hurt my standing here, either, she thought. She cocked her head, eyeing him curiously. "Why... did you do that?"

"It seemed the least I could do after getting you in so much hot water. I probably shouldn't have called when you were on the air. But it hit me wrong when you read the news release. I—" He shrugged, running a hand through his hair. "Sometimes I do impulsive things."

So do I, she thought. How could she possibly be angry with him now? She realized she was smiling.

He glanced around the small control room with obvious interest, appraising the equipment. "I haven't been in a radio station in years. This is fascinating. All right if I stay for a few minutes and watch?" Instinctively, she shook her head, and he raised one large palm as if stopping traffic.

"Okay. I understand. But before you kick me out, let me ask one favor." He reached into his shirt pocket and pulled out a white card. "I just happen to have a pass for a free dinner for two at—"

"Maximillian's," she finished for him.

His dark green eyes caught her gaze and held it. "Will you have dinner with me tonight?"

"I can't." Long years of refusing invitations conditioned her response. The words escaped before Desiree could stop them.

"Why not?"

"Because I . . ." she began, then paused in confusion.

He's a wealthy entrepreneur from Seattle, she cautioned herself. You're a deejay in cutoffs from Anaheim. He's only asking you out because you're convenient, and he has a free dinner and no one to share it with.

"I . . ." She'd always been the master of the instant fabricated excuse. Why couldn't she think of anything? "I have plans," she finished lamely.

"Oh." He nodded slowly, then leaned forward, gazing at her, his elbow on the counter and his chin resting on his hand. "I guess I shouldn't have expected you to be available on the spur of the moment. But I had to give it a try."

Inexplicably, a wave of disappointment welled up in Desiree's stomach. Was he going to give up so easily?

"Still, maybe we can work something out. These plans of yours. Tell me about them."

"Well—" Don't you have eyes? a small voice taunted in the back of her mind. The man's an eleven on a scale of ten! What are you waiting for?

"I promise you I'm harmless." He flashed her a boyish grin, raising his right hand in the traditional Boy Scout salute. "Trustworthy, honest and obedient. Scout's honor."

She couldn't stop her laugh. His smile radiated warmth and friendliness. You'll like me, it said. I already like you. She paused a moment, admiring his high sculpted cheekbones and the fine laugh lines at the corners of his eyes. When her gaze rested on the gracefully angled bridge of his nose, she fought a sudden urge to run her finger down its narrow tanned slope to the place near the tip where it dipped and turned up just the tiniest bit.

"Is it anything of critical importance?" he persisted. "Or could you get out of it?"

"I'm not sure if..." Her voice trailed off. Why not go out with him? She hated to play right into Barbara's hands, but maybe her friend was right. She ought to enjoy some male company for a change. Since he lived so far away, it would be all on her own terms. Dinner only, with no danger of involvement and no strings attached.

She looked him straight in the eye. "I was going to fly to Washington for a late supper with the President, but I suppose I could call and cancel."

He pushed himself off the counter with a roar of deep sparkling laughter. The delightful sound ricocheted off the walls of the small room, sending shock waves spiraling through Desiree's body. "Dinner at the White House! Is that all? And here I was afraid it was something really special!"

She shrugged, smiling. "You're right. That kind of invitation is rather run-of-the-mill. I'll say something's come up and I can't make it. I mean, let's keep our priorities straight. How often do I have the opportunity to dine with a soda-pop king?"

Kyle waited for her in the lobby until her shift ended at six o'clock. Fortunately, she found Barbara had gone for the day. Questions would certainly come tomorrow, but for now she was spared the embarrassment of a confrontation.

He followed in his car as she drove to her three-bedroom tract house in Anaheim to change her clothes for dinner. As he stood behind her on the front stoop, Desiree unlocked the door and pushed it open a crack. She peered through the small opening into her living room, unsure in what condition she'd left the place. Cheeks flaming, she whirled around, yanking the door shut behind her. Her body collided with his in a sudden sharp impact, completely knocking the breath from her.

"Oh! I'm sorry!" Kyle grabbed her by the shoulders, not retreating an inch.

"You can't go in there," she gasped. She stood pinned between him and the door, staring directly at the magnificent tangle of dark-brown hair at the base of his throat.

"Why not?" His hands gripped her shoulders firmly as he looked down at her.

"It's a battlefield. Several people died there this morning, and the bodies haven't been cleared away yet."

He laughed. "I'm sure I've seen worse. Don't worry about it."

He stood so close she felt the warmth emanating from his body, felt his breath, warm and sweet, on her cheek. She pressed her back against the door, tilted her head back slightly and looked up at him. "Impossible. Take my word for it, this is worse than anything you could possibly imagine."

"It doesn't matter. I didn't exactly give you much warning. I don't expect a red carpet and champagne." His eyes roved slowly over her face, lingering for a long moment at her lips as if they were a mouth-watering dessert just out of his reach. His voice was somewhat rough when he spoke again. "I came to see you, not the way you keep house."

Her shoulders, under the pressure of his fingers, began to tingle, sending magnificent shooting sparks throughout her body. She was aware for the first time of the faint scent of a very pleasant masculine cologne. She closed her eyes, wanting him to keep holding her forever. If only her living room wasn't such a mess then he could come inside. She'd like to have him in her house. In her living room. In her bedroom. In her—

No, Desiree! she cautioned. He's gorgeous and witty and incredibly sexy, but for God's sake, don't get carried away. Tomorrow he'll fly back to his work and his life in Seattle, and you'll be back to your comfortable, uncomplicated routine. Your comfortable, uncomplicated, boring, lonely routine.

She took a deep breath. "Yes, but there's . . . the dog."

He relaxed his grip on her shoulders and stepped back. "The dog?"

"The dog. A vicious Doberman. Trained to attack strange men on sight."

"I'm not strange. And I love dogs." He studied her for a moment with narrowed eyes, a smile playing at the corners of his lips. "Would it really embarrass you that much if I saw the way you keep house?"

"It really would."

"Why?"

"Because..." She hesitated, her shoulders still tingling from the remembered pressure of his fingers. "I don't want you to think—"

"Think what?"

She sighed in resignation. "That I'm a slob."

"I won't think that. I'll keep an open mind. I promise." And with one quick deft movement he reached around her waist, turned the knob and pushed the door wide open.

She could have died. She wished she wasn't so disorderly; she preferred tabletops and counters to be clear and things to be organized and put in their places. She just couldn't seem to get herself to do it on a regular basis.

Several discarded sweaters lay draped across the back of the flowered chintz sofa and matching love seat. A wing chair in a French blue-and-apricot print held clean laundry waiting to be folded. To her mortification a pair of sheer panties and a lacy bra peeked out quite noticeably from the center of the pile.

Numerous pairs of shoes and sandals lay under the antique mahogany coffee table and at either side of the couch and chairs. Magazines and books lay scattered on every surface, and partially filled water glasses on cork coasters seemed to be everywhere—on the ornate carved credenza, on top of the lawyer's bookcase, even on the mantel over the brick fireplace.

Gritting her teeth, her stomach quietly tying itself in knots, Desiree stepped inside. When would she grow out of that habit of taking a glass of water with her everywhere she went? And when would she learn to stop taking her shoes off and leaving them wherever she happened to be sitting? What was this man going to think of her?

Kyle took a step inside and shoved his hands in his pockets, his lips set in a fixed noncommittal line. The expression in his dark green eyes as they swept the cluttered room could only be called dismay. When she saw his gaze drift to the kitchen, where she'd stacked last night's dinner dishes and pots on the Formica counter, the color rose in her cheeks.

"I knew it," she said. "You're a neat freak. One of those folds-his-underwear-in-the-drawer types."

He nodded his head slowly, wordlessly.

"I was afraid of that." She wanted to disappear into thin air, to start the day over again. She scooped an armful of sweaters off the sofa and crumpled them into a tight ball against her thudding chest.

Any kind of relationship, even a short-term one, wasn't supposed to begin this way. A man, on seeing a woman's home for the first time, was supposed to be overwhelmed by its charm, impressed by her impeccable taste in furniture and decor. Well, she'd certainly impressed him. He was speechless!

"I told you it'd be a disaster," she said. "I'm sorry. It's not always this bad."

He laughed lightly. "It's okay. It makes me feel right at home. Really. I have five sisters. To this day, every one of them is a bit . . . relaxed about keeping house, you might say."

"Five sisters? How on earth—" did you ever turn out so incredibly, indisputably masculine, she wanted to say "—did you ever survive?" she finished quickly.

"As a matter of fact, it worked out rather well. Being the only son, I got royal treatment. My own room. Special outings with my dad. It was great."

She smiled, grateful for his easygoing manner and apparently intentional effort to change the subject. "I just have one brother. I'll bet growing up in a big family was a lot of fun."

"It *was* fun." He sat down on the edge of the couch and absently arranged the scattered magazines and books into neat stacks. "I enjoyed playing Big Brother to a house full of beautiful women. The girls are terrific. All of them, especially the twins."

"Twins! How wonderful. I used to dream I'd have twins of my own some day." Her eyes swept to his chest. Firm pectoral muscles rippled in sharp relief beneath the thin white summer dress shirt. A shadow of dark chest hair stretched across his upper torso. Her breasts began to tingle as she imagined the trail of curly hair leading down from his chest, across his flat stomach, narrowing to a thin satiny line as it descended to . . .

"Maybe you will." His voice brought her eyes up to meet his with a guilty start. Maybe she would what?

She stepped over to the credenza and turned on her stereo, letting the soft music of KICK-FM fill the room. "I hope you like mellow music."

"If I don't, I think I'm taking out the wrong girl."

She returned his smile. "You have a point there."

He ran his fingers along the carved leg of the coffee table. "Your furniture is beautiful. Is this an antique?"

She nodded. "It belonged to my great-grandmother. All of this did. Do you like antiques?"

"I usually go for the more modern stuff but I admire the craftsmanship on these old pieces. Especially the hand carving."

"If you like carving, you should see the incredible detail work on my four-poster bed. It's—" She broke off. Why did she say that? It almost sounded like an invitation!

His eyes lit up. "I'd love to see it."

"No!" She realized she had shouted the word and tried to soften her voice. "Sorry. The bedroom's even more of a disaster than the living room. I couldn't possibly let you in there." She took several steps backward. "I'll go and change. Oh, can I get you something to drink?"

"No, thanks." He indicated a half-filled water glass on the coffee table. "I'll just help myself to some of this if I get thirsty."

She choked back an embarrassed laugh. "Try the one on the credenza. It's probably fresher." Turning, she fled down the hall. If she survived this evening with her sanity intact, it'd be a miracle.

She was only going out with this man once, so she might as well do it right, Desiree thought as she fastened the tiny buttons up the front of her lavender cotton sundress. What was it Barbara said? In the right dress... with your hair up... you'd be as glamorous as hell. Well, the dress was far from glamorous, but it was the best she could do. The flared skirt, trimmed at the hem by a long ruffle with matching crocheted lace, made her feel dainty and feminine, and the form-fitting bodice accentuated her tiny waistline. The deep orchid color contrasted with her fair complexion and brought a vibrant healthy glow to her face.

She pulled on high-heeled white sandals and picked up her brush from the antique dresser, running it fiercely through the light brown curls that cascaded over her shoulders. She never wore her hair up. How would it look? She threw her head forward, grabbed the thick mass of hair and twisted it into a bun on top of her head. Holding the bulky knot in place with one hand, she pulled a few wispy tendrils of hair down around her forehead and ears. Standing up, she surveyed the effect in the beveled mirror above her dresser.

She looked ridiculous. Like a midget balancing a ball on her head. *Face it. You'll never get Miss America out of a Kewpie doll.*

Sighing, she shook her head vigorously, letting the gleaming waves fall into place in their natural side part, then clipped them back above each ear with gold barrettes. On a sudden impulse, she pulled out a delicate gold pendant from her jewelry box and fastened it around her neck.

When she returned to the living room, she found Kyle thumbing through a magazine, one arm draped across the back of the sofa, his legs stretched out in front of him. He'd buttoned his shirt and had put on a handsome brown-and-blue-striped tie, which he must have brought in from his car. The last beams of fading sunlight streaming in through the front window burnished the gleaming bronze and copper highlights in his hair. He looked totally natural and completely at ease, as if he made a daily habit of waiting in strange women's living rooms while they dressed for dinner. As she wondered if that was true, she thought he looked right somehow, relaxing there on her couch, as if he belonged there.

She smiled. "Glad to see you made yourself at home."

He tossed the magazine aside and looked up at her, his eyebrows lifting in admiration. He let out a low whistle. "Wow! You look terrific. I like your dress."

"This dress?" She felt her cheeks glow with pleasure, but couldn't quite bring herself to meet his gaze. Fingering a corner of the long ruffled hem, she said, "It's just an old thing. I'm sorry I don't have something more . . . chic, but—"

"You mean something in electric-blue silk, open in the back, cut off the shoulder?"

The color in her cheeks deepened. "Something like that."

"Sounds too flashy to me. I prefer what you're wearing. It shows off your beautiful figure." He sprang up off the sofa with an athletic grace and covered the distance between them in a few quick strides. Tilting his head to one side, he regarded her the way an artist might study a painting. "That's a beautiful pendant."

"Thank you." She fingered the golden charm at her throat. Her favorite piece of jewelry, it depicted a tiny robin perched on a branch, singing its heart out to the sky. A small diamond twinkled in its eye.

"A songbird," he said. "Just like you." His admiring gaze brought a golden gleam to her eyes and she smiled.

"With your hair pulled back like that, you should be wearing earrings," he said. "Something gold and sparkling, to match the pendant."

"That might pose a little problem. This is over a hundred and fifty years old. I doubt they'd make anything to match it now."

"I should have guessed. An antique. From your great-grandmother, I suppose?"

She nodded. "From my great-grandmother. I was named after her, and was lucky enough to get some of her prize possessions."

"Well, she had excellent taste in furniture and jewelry. And in great-granddaughters." He lifted one hand to the slope of her neck, sifted his fingers through her hair and held it up to the light, watching as the gleaming strands fell softly back to her shoulders. He stared down at her for a long moment, his hand poised in midair, fingers tense and contracting, as if fighting a silent war within himself.

Adrenaline pumped through Desiree's body as her eyes locked with his. What was going on in his mind? Why was he staring at her like that? A shiver tiptoed up her spine and her pulse quickened, as if anticipating a plunge into deep icy waters. She blinked and lowered her eyes to his full, beautifully shaped lips. For some reason her thoughts scattered like petals in the wind and she struggled to reorganize them.

He shoved his hands in his pockets and took a step back. She sighed with relief. Or was it regret?

"What do you say we go eat?" he said. "I'm starving."

Three

———

They sat at a window-side table, overlooking the wide expanse of white beach and rolling surf one flight of stairs below. Desiree had never been inside Maximillian's, although she'd often admired its stunning blend of plate glass and California redwood when she passed by during an evening walk on the Huntington Beach pier. The interior was both comfortable and sophisticated with its nautical theme, tables draped in royal-blue, solid oak chairs and vases of chrysanthemums scattered about.

She'd noticed several women's heads turn as she and Kyle made their way through the crowded restaurant to their table. No wonder. Kyle was easily the best-looking man in the room.

Their conversation flowed as smooth as the wine. The waiter, when he stopped to take their order, apologized for intruding, which made them laugh. Kyle seemed to want to know everything about her, and she was equally fascinated by him, each new and exciting detail of his life only whetting her appetite to learn more.

"How long have you been working at KICK?" Kyle asked after the waiter had served bowls of thick clam chowder.

"Two years."

"I read a review of your show in the *Times* on the flight down this morning. You're quite a celebrity."

"Not really." She shrugged. "It's a pretty small station. Few people recognize me by voice, and nobody knows me by sight. Thank goodness."

"What do you mean, thank goodness?" Kyle held his wineglass to his lips, inhaling its bouquet. "I thought all performers liked to be recognized."

"Not me. My voice...I'm sure you've noticed. It's so...low. It doesn't match up with the rest of me. People have kidded me about it since I was twelve. My listeners seem to expect some blond curvaceous beauty. You can imagine how disappointed they are when they meet me."

He fell silent, watching her. "I wasn't disappointed," he said softly.

She felt a flutter in her stomach and wanted to look away, but couldn't bring herself to break their eye contact. "You ... weren't?"

He shook his head. "I think your voice fits you perfectly." He seemed to want to say more. She held her breath, waiting, wondering how she'd respond if he told her she was beautiful. She knew she wasn't, even though other people seemed determined to convince her she was. Would she believe it, if he said the words?

He glanced away. She swallowed the disappointment that welled in her throat.

"While you were getting dressed, I took a look at your library," he said, picking up his knife and spreading sweet butter thickly on a chunk of crusty sourdough bread. "Very impressive."

"My library?" She let go a short laugh. "You mean the books piled on the coffee table, or the ones stacked three-deep on the shelves?"

"Both. We seem to collect the same books. I saw quite a few of my favorite authors and titles: Maxine O'Callaghan and T. Jefferson Parker."

"I love their stuff!" She smiled with delight as she took a spoonful of chowder. "My problem is I end up keeping them all. I ran out of shelf space long ago, but books are like best friends. I can't stand to part with any of them."

"Me neither. But I've got more space than you. My whole living room's lined with bookshelves. Reading's the best kind of company for someone living alone."

She nodded. "I know what you mean. Keeps me from noticing how lonely I am. I read while I eat, before I go to sleep—"

"It does get lonely, doesn't it?"

She froze, her spoon halfway to her mouth. His eyes locked with hers across the table.

"Do you like living alone?" he asked softly.

A current of awareness seemed to travel across the space between them. She lowered her eyes, toyed with the blue linen napkin in her lap. "I . . . don't mind it. I've been alone for five years. I guess I'm used to it by now." She laughed lightly. "I'd better be used to it, anyway. I don't have any choice. I tried marriage once. It didn't even last a year. I'll never try it again."

"Never say *never*. You can't tell who you'll meet. Maybe you just married the wrong man."

"I don't think so. The divorce was inevitable, no matter who I'd married." She hoped he wouldn't pursue the subject further. She considered the last months before the divorce to be the lowest point in her life. She preferred to forget them.

"How about you?" she asked. "Have you ever been married?"

"No."

"Really? Thirty-two years old and never been hitched?"

A smile tugged at the corners of his lips. "Thirty-five. But thanks for the compliment."

She expected him to add more, to explain that he, too, was against the idea of marriage. After all, she reasoned, a man this handsome, this charming and successful, could hardly have escaped marriage unless he had an aversion to the institution in general. But he said nothing for several heartbeats, just continued to look at her over the rim of his wineglass.

She felt her skin grow hot under his searing gaze and she glanced out the window beside them, where the setting sun painted a watercolor wash of purple, pink and gold across the sky. A few hardy surfers still sat astride their boards, rising and falling on the water's dark surface like bobbing ducks.

"I guess we can't get married, anyway," he said.

Her eyes flew up to meet his.

"We'd have two copies of every book in the house."

His sudden drop in tone made her heart race. "True. It'd create . . . a definite storage problem."

She had no idea what to say next. To her relief the waiter chose that moment to arrive with their dinners. For Desiree, a platter of mesquite-broiled halibut, with wild rice, french-cut green beans and honeyed carrots on the side. When the waiter placed Kyle's meal before him, she felt a pang of envy rise in her chest. He'd ordered lobster. Fresh American lobster, flown in that morning from Maine.

"Ahh. Look at this beauty." Kyle spread his cloth napkin across his lap. The lobster reclined on a bed of rice in reddish-orange splendor, head and tail intact, arched shell up. The detached claws, already cracked, were arranged beside a cup of melted butter. She could smell its rich scent across the table.

She watched him pierce a wedge of lemon with his fork and squeeze it into the butter. Her mouth watered. He used the fork to scoop a large piece of white meat from one claw, dipped it into the lemon butter and lifted it to his lips. He caught her eye and stopped, the fork poised in midair.

"I *told* you to order the lobster," he said.

It was true. The waiter had also highly recommended it. But the complimentary dinner pass stated plainly that lobster was not included. Favorite food or no, they came for a free dinner, and she insisted at least one of them should take advantage of it. Besides, she could eat for half a week for the same price.

"This is fine," she said. She quickly tasted a piece of halibut. Firm. Meaty. Dry. One hundred and ninety-four calories per four ounce serving. "Delicious," she lied.

"Try this." Kyle extended his forkful of lobster across the table.

"Your first bite? No, I couldn't—" Before she could protest further, he popped the morsel into her mouth. She closed her eyes and chewed, savoring the moist buttery flavor.

"Oh, yum," she said. "A rare treat. It's been ages." She heard his laugh, followed by a scraping sound. When she blinked open her eyes, the lobster stared back at her. Her own plate sat in front of Kyle.

"I got a sudden uncontrollable craving for halibut." He picked up the plastic bib the waiter had brought, leaned forward and tied it around Desiree's neck. "This looks better on you than it would on me, anyway."

Her eyes widened. "No, Kyle. I wouldn't dream of...are you sure you don't mind?"

"Go ahead. Enjoy."

She pounced. Picking up the lobster's steaming shell in two hands, she turned it soft side up and arched it until the tail-piece pulled loose from the body. With one deft movement she bent back the tail flipper section until it cracked off. She lifted the tailpiece downside up, expertly inserted the lobster fork through the hole left by the flippers and pushed the tail meat out through the open end.

"I can see," he said, watching her, "just how rarely you get lobster."

"It's only been rare recently." She took a bite, paused for a moment of appreciative silence. "I lived in Maine for a year and a half. Every chance I got I'd drive down to Bar Harbor and buy a lobster at the wharf. Three dollars a pound, plucked right out of the tank and cooked while you wait."

His eyes never left her face. "No wonder you can't stand the prices here."

She broke off one of the lobster's legs, softly closed her mouth around the open end. With lips and tongue she slowly and gently sucked out the contents. Across from her and watching, Kyle drew a single breath that was out of rhythm with the others. His green eyes glittered with sudden brightness, and a smile lingered on his mouth. All at once aware of what he might be thinking, Desiree felt her cheeks flush red and hot. She swallowed hard. Picking up one of the legs, she held it out to him. "Would you ... like to share?"

He shook his head, eyes still locked with hers. "Not . . . just now." Finally he picked up his knife and fork.

As they enjoyed the meal, they talked. Desiree found herself relaxing as he skillfully directed the conversation from one topic to another. They discovered they liked the same movies, listened to the same music, and both enjoyed the theater. She told him about the wonderful Victorian house in Pasadena where she grew up, how sad she'd been when her parents sold it and moved to Florida.

Kyle had lived in Seattle all of his life, he said. His parents and most of his relatives still lived there.

"Washington's beautiful. Everything's green all year round. From my office window on the tenth floor I've got a fantastic view of downtown and Elliot Bay. When the sun shines the sky is the bluest blue you've ever seen."

"Have you been to Southern California before?" she asked.

"A few times. It's too hot for me. And smoggy."

"Not always. Today you could have fried pancakes on the curb but try coming down in spring or winter. I'll bet our sky's as blue as yours."

"I've seen days where it comes close," he admitted. "But I'd still never trade Washington for this zoo." He folded his napkin on the table and sat back in his chair. "I take it you like it here?"

"Love it. After a few summers in Tucson and winters in Detroit and Bangor, Maine, I'll take this weather any day. Wild brontosauruses couldn't drag me away from this place now, especially since I got my own 'drive time' show. Seven years of nights is enough for anyone."

"Why'd it take so long to get a decent shift?"

"There's a built-in prejudice in this business against women. For the past twenty years, we've been stuck with the worst hours for the least pay. Midnight to dawn—they still call it the Women's Shift. And that's one of the nicer names for it." Five years ago, she explained, you rarely heard a woman on the air during the afternoon, even in Southern California. "They're a bit more progressive here. Most deejays would kill for the chance to work in L.A. or Orange County. It's the hottest market in the country."

"Why? Because you're so close to the television and film industries?"

"That's a big part of it. A jock with a good voice can earn a lot of money on the side in commercials, voice-overs, cartoons. But the biggest attraction here is the pay scale." She finished her wine. With instinctive awareness Kyle reached for the bottle in the ice bucket and raised an eyebrow in her direction. At her nod, he refilled her glass.

"AFTRA, our union, takes care of us," she went on. "Sees to it we have decent wages and working conditions. Other markets aren't so lucky. Just a few years back I was working ridiculous hours for starvation wages."

"Really? I imagined deejays were paid handsomely. Like TV stars."

"Far from it. This might be show biz, but we're the bottom of the scale."

She reached across the table to offer him her last bite of lobster. He smiled and leaned forward, then closed his lips around her fork. At the same time his hand closed around hers. A spark shot through her veins at the warmth of his touch.

"Good," he said, his eyes lighting up appreciatively. She wasn't sure if he was referring to the taste of the food or the feel of her hand. He took the fork from her and set it down, leaned her elbows on the table and wrapped her hand in both of his. "Why have you lived in so many places? Detroit, did you say? Tucson? And Maine?"

"Change of jobs." His hands, she noticed, were tanned and covered with dark springy hairs. They felt warm and dry and wonderful against hers. "In this business after a year at the same station you're practically considered an old-timer. Unemployment's always looking over your shoulder."

"Why is it so hard to keep a job?"

"Ratings."

The candlelight flickered across the side of his face and caught in minute flashes the reddish-gold of his day's growth of whiskers. She wondered if his cheeks felt smooth or rough to the touch. She wondered what color his beard would be. Brown? Or bright red, like the highlights in his hair?

"Ratings?" he asked.

She took a deep breath and continued. "If the station isn't doing well, the program director often wipes the slate clean and starts off with all new talent. Or he might decide to switch the format of the station from music to Talk Radio or All News, which also requires a whole new crop of people. And there are so many young kids, beating down the door to take our jobs. If we forget to play one spot or say one thing the P.D. doesn't like, he might decide to can us, try somebody else."

"Sounds too precarious for my blood," he said.

"Not me. Once you're in the business, it's like a compulsion. Any other job would pale in comparison."

She watched, transfixed, as his fingers gently rubbed across the back of her knuckles. The tingling sensations that began there raced the length of her arm, down through her body. She wondered what it would feel like if his fingers were to touch her in more intimate places, in places that had been so long denied, and even now seemed to swell with—

She tore her eyes away and looked down at the table, drawing a mental curtain over the dangerous pictures forming in her mind. To her surprise their plates were gone, replaced by steaming cups of coffee. When had the busboy stopped by?

"Cream?" he asked, letting go of her hand.

"Y...yes," she managed in a strangled voice. Stop thinking of him that way, she scolded herself. You'll drive yourself crazy.

She took the pitcher of cream from him and allowed herself a small dab. "We've talked far too much about me. Tell me, how'd you come to be such a power in the business world?"

He answered her questions simply, but with enthusiasm. He seemed proud of his achievements, and showed no trace of conceit or arrogance. He studied engineering in college, he told her, worked for a while at Boeing and eventually decided to start his own company to manufacture tooling and parts for aircraft. The business mushroomed after a few years, and he invested in other companies, including an engineering firm. Sparkle Light was his latest acquisition.

"Why a soft-drink company?" she asked, after a rather bemused busboy had refilled their coffee cups for the third time.

"Everything else is related to aerospace. It doesn't seem to fit in."

He shrugged. "It looked profitable. Keeps things interesting."

"And you started the whole thing on a shoestring." She shook her head in amazement. "I'll bet when the other kids were playing cops and robbers, you were out learning how to close business deals."

He didn't answer right away. Instead, he gazed out the window at the midnight-blue sky, which descended toward the rippling dark water in gradually lighter shades of blue.

"To tell you the truth, I never intended to go into business at all," he said in a low voice. "From the time I saw Cary Grant in *Only Angels Have Wings*, all I ever wanted to do was fly airplanes. As a kid I was crazy about airplanes, helicopters, spaceships—anything that flew. I made models, read every book I could find on the subject. Vowed I'd someday be a commercial pilot or join the air force."

"So that's how you knew the answer to that obscure trivia question about the helicopter! I thought for sure I had you stumped on that one."

He grinned and reached for her hand again across the table. "Lucky for me I got it right."

Why did she feel such a sizzling jolt each time he touched her hand? "Then why didn't you become a pilot? What happened to change your mind?"

"I didn't change my mind." To her surprise and disappointment he jerked his hand away. "Certain circumstances prevented me from becoming a pilot. I thought designing airplanes would be an acceptable substitute for flying them, but it didn't work out that way." He remained silent, staring moodily into his empty coffee cup.

She read resentment and suppressed frustration in his gaze. Her fingers ached to reach out and touch his cheek, to smooth away the lines of tension she saw there. As she debated the advisability of such a move, he abruptly pushed back his chair and stood up.

"Well, what do you say we go, before they start charging us rent for this table?" Kyle said as he paid the check.

Desiree fumbled for her purse and quickly followed Kyle out
of the restaurant. Conversation was strained during the twenty-
minute drive back to her house.

She sank back into the Maserati's deep leather-cushioned seat
and watched the darkened rows of stucco housing tracts whiz
by. What prevented Kyle from becoming·a pilot, she wondered. He'd been so free to tell her everything else about himself. Why did he suddenly become withdrawn when that subject
was brought up?

He pulled into her driveway, got out and walked her to her
front step.

Her palms began to perspire. Should she ask him in? No, too
dangerous. It would sound like an invitation for something
more. She reached into her purse, pulled out her key. "Well,
good night, Kyle. Thank you for—"

"Wait." He placed one hand on her arm and plucked the
house keys from her with the other. "Do you know why I came
to the station tonight?"

Her eyes lifted in surprise. "To pick up the free dinner pass."
As soon as she said it she realized how ridiculous it sounded.
What did a man like Kyle need with a free dinner pass?

"That was just an excuse. I came to meet you."

"Oh," she said, feeling flattered and flustered at the same
time.

"When I heard you on the radio, I kept wondering what you
looked like," he said, fingering the keys in his hand. "I couldn't
stop thinking about you. I wanted to know if there was a living breathing woman behind the sexy voice."

His reference to her on-air role made her blush. "It's not
really me, you know. It's just a part I play. I do it because my
program director likes it. It keeps the ratings up."

"No need to defend yourself. I think it's great. I'll bet every
red-blooded male in Southern California feels the same way.
You must get hundreds of calls every week—bags of mail."

"I get my share. Seems like every night there's some guy
hanging around outside the station at the end of my shift,
waiting to offer me a ride home."

He placed his hands on her waist. "Ever take anyone up on
it?"

Her breasts began to tremble from the sudden erratic beating of her heart. "Never."

"Never?"

She shook her head. He was standing so very close. The heat from his hands was a sizzling presence at her sides. She wanted to wind her hands around his neck and pull him against her, until she could feel the warmth of his body against hers.

"Heartless woman," he growled.

She swallowed hard. "Not really. I don't meet them too often. I usually work very late."

He laughed. "Exactly what your receptionist told me. 'If she finds out you're here, she'll hide in the studio until ten o'clock. You'd better just go barge in.' So I did. I hope you didn't mind."

"I didn't."

His hand slipped from her waist to the small of her back and drew her to him. A tremor ran through her as her softness molded against the hard contours of his thighs and chest. He lifted his hand and gently grazed his fingertips up the soft whiteness of her neck to rest briefly on her earlobe. He held her gaze for a moment, his eyes smoldering in the reflected glow of a nearby street lamp.

Her heart pounded in her ears. She knew he wanted to kiss her. And she knew now that she'd dreamed of his kiss, hungered for it, from the moment they first met. But she couldn't let it happen. The magnetic pull she felt toward him was overpowering. The very touch of his hand had caused fire to rush through her veins, threatening to consume her with need. Once she felt his mouth on hers, she'd be lost.

He was only here for a day or two. There was no telling if he'd be back. And she couldn't get involved with Kyle, with any man, even if he lived next door. How long would she be at KICK? Another year, maybe two? Then, as always, she'd have to move on. She could never stay in one city long enough to make a relationship last.

Kyle Harrison already lived more than a thousand miles away. No matter how strong her attraction to him, she knew that long-distance relationships didn't work. She'd been through it before with Steve, and her heart still hadn't quite mended. It would be emotional suicide to try it again.

"I've got to go. It's getting late." She tried to pull free of his embrace but his arms tightened around her.

"Is it?"

"Yes. I have to get to the station early tomorrow. And you must have a long drive back to your hotel."

His body moved against her as he shrugged. "Maybe."

"What do you mean?" she asked in sudden alarm. "Don't you have a place to stay?"

He shook his head. "I had reservations at a hotel outside of L.A., was on my way there from my meeting when I heard you on the radio." A light gleamed in his eyes. "I got kind of side-tracked."

She wrenched herself out of his arms and stepped back, panic rising in her throat. Did he think she'd let him stay here? "I'm sure the hotel held your reservation. You can call them to see. And if not you can check the phone book for—"

"Relax." He shoved his hands in his pockets, his eyes narrowing as he watched her. "I'll find a room somewhere."

She let out a relieved breath. "Well, then. Do you want to use my phone?"

"No. Don't worry about it." He made no move to leave.

"How long did you say you're here for?"

"Two days. I go back tomorrow afternoon."

"Oh."

"Can I call you sometime? After I get back to Seattle?"

"Sure," she said, knowing he wouldn't.

"Good." He reached for her hand, turned it over and dropped her keys into her palm. She climbed the step and unlocked the door, her heart still pumping erratically. This is what she wanted, wasn't it? A quick and final goodbye?

"Thanks for having dinner with me," he said. "I enjoyed it."

She turned back to face him, one hand on the doorknob. She wanted to tell him how much she'd enjoyed his company, that she'd like to see him again, even though she knew it would never happen and would be hopeless even if it did. She opened her mouth to speak, then shut it again.

"Good night," he said.
Goodbye, she amended silently.
He turned on his heel and was gone.

Four

Desiree slept badly. What little sleep she managed to catch was filled with dreams of Kyle. She went through her morning aerobics routine and fixed her usual breakfast—half a grapefruit, a poached egg, a cup of black coffee—but she couldn't seem to get him out of her mind. One date, that's all it was, she reminded herself. That's the only reason you went. No danger of involvement. No strings attached.

Hah, she thought as she rinsed off yesterday's stack of dishes and slid them into the dishwasher. So much for not getting involved. So much for no strings attached. From the moment they met she'd felt a wild attraction to the man and she couldn't do a thing about it.

Activity, she told herself. That's what you need. Anything to get your mind off Kyle. All at once the clutter in her house seemed a welcome challenge. She spent the better part of the morning clearing away the scattered books and clothes in the living room, vacuuming and dusting, even scrubbing the kitchen floor. The bedroom was still a mess, but it would have to wait. Shortly before noon, pleased with her accomplishments, she locked up and left for work.

She slipped through the side door at the station, hoping Barbara was too busy to bother her. No such luck. Desiree had just begun taping a routine for her Comedy Corner series when Barbara strode through the recording-studio door.

"Des! There you are. I've been dying to hear—" Barbara stopped short at Desiree's forlorn expression. "What happened? Didn't you go out with him?"

"Yes."

"And?"

"Leave me alone."

"What do you mean, leave me alone? I have to know! What happened?"

"We went out to dinner. Then he took me home."

"That's it?"

"That's it."

"Good grief, why didn't you ask him in? Was he a creep or something?"

"No," Desiree snapped. "He wasn't a creep."

"Then why... You're going to see him again, aren't you?"

Desiree let out a long sigh. "How do you suggest I do that? He lives in Seattle."

"So what? That's what airports are for. Geez, Des, the man was gorgeous. I thought for sure you'd go nuts over him. And he was so nice, the way he fixed things with Sam." She looked at Desiree anxiously. "You aren't mad at me, are you? For sending him back to see you yesterday?"

Desiree shrugged. "I'm not mad. I just don't want to talk about it. Okay?"

Barbara's hands flew up in exasperation. "You're impossible." She turned to leave, nearly colliding with an enormous arrangement of long-stemmed red roses carried aloft in the doorway.

"Are these for me?" Barbara cried.

"Sorry, sweetheart." Tom peered around the flowers and grinned at Desiree. "They're for the lovely lady in the cutoffs and white T-shirt. Better tell me where you want 'em pronto, 'cause this thing weighs a ton."

Desiree stared at the brilliant red buds. There must have been three dozen, surrounded by ferns and baby's breath in a tall cut-glass vase. She squeezed in front of Barbara and grabbed the small attached envelope. Turning her back, she pulled out the card inside. It read simply: *To the loveliest woman I've ever shared a lobster with. Kyle.*

Her stomach seemed to trip over itself. She realized she'd been holding her breath and let it out in a long deep sigh. Aware of Barbara's tall form peering over her shoulder, she clasped the card to her chest. "This is private, if you don't mind."

"Just went out to dinner, huh? Never going to see him again?" Smirking with satisfaction, Barbara tossed her dark hair and slipped out the door.

"If you don't tell me where to put these, I'm going to dump them right here so they can get used for a doorstop," Tom said.

"Sorry. I'll take them."

Tom lowered the heavy vase into Desiree's arms, and she inhaled the sweet fragrance of a perfect red bud.

"What happened, anyway?" Tom said. "Did somebody die?" At her withering glare he grinned and ducked into the hallway.

Just after 3:00 P.M. Desiree glanced up at the clock. How could only two minutes have gone by since she last checked the time? The day usually zoomed by for her. Today time crawled. The roses' perfume filled the small studio, doing nothing to decrease the feeling of light-headedness that had descended on her the moment they arrived.

She wondered what time Kyle's plane left for Seattle. Was he still in the meeting? Had he already gone? Would he call before he left?

She wanted to thank him for the flowers, but realized she'd never even asked for his home address or phone number. Should she call information or leave a message at his office?

It was impossible to concentrate. Memories of the way he had looked across the dinner table by candlelight, the intimate way he'd held her hand, the look in his eyes when he had leaned against the front door that afternoon, played over and over in her mind like a movie on a continuous reel. Several times she found herself singing along with the music. She'd forget to notice when a song began to fade and nearly miss her cue for the next tune.

She forgot to keep track of what she played and couldn't think of a single witty thing to say. The Trivia Game contest was completely lacking in excitement. She dutifully screened each call, her heart leaping with each punch of the button, hoping it might be Kyle. It wasn't. The man she finally put on the air stuttered and stammered and was about as lively as a dead chicken.

Somehow she managed to finish her shift. At six o'clock, she strolled nonchalantly into the reception area and asked if anyone had called or come by.

"Sorry," Barbara said as she packed up to leave. "His Gorgeousness has not appeared within these four walls. Better luck tomorrow."

Disappointment curled inside her stomach like a tightly wound spring. He'd left without saying goodbye.

She retreated to the recording studio, began to dub comedy spots and humorous sound effects from albums onto tape. Between seven and eight someone dropped off a hamburger and fries, and she dug into it hungrily. By nine-thirty the effects of her long day had caught up with her. Feeling tired and dejected, she returned the albums to the station's library, grabbed her purse and sweater and headed for home.

She parked in her garage and was in the process of yanking down the heavy wood door when she heard the approaching roar of a car. Tires squealed. A dark-green Maserati turned into her driveway and stopped before her, engine humming, headlights glaring.

Kyle leaned his head out the open car window. "Just getting home?"

Astonishment and excitement tingled through her at the same time. She couldn't believe how glad she was to see him. Glad? she asked herself. Understatement of the year. Try ecstatic.

She locked the garage door and crossed to his car, fighting to keep back the smile threatening to curve her lips. The smile won. "Broads in broadcasting are dedicated souls," she said.

"No kidding. Remind me to believe you if you ever say you have to work late."

She leaned on the window frame. In the glow of the street lamp she could see he wore a pale gray and white pin-striped suit, light blue shirt and matching striped tie. He looked gorgeous.

"Thanks for the roses," she said. "They're beautiful."

"My pleasure."

His rusty-brown hair was wind-tousled. She ached to run her fingers through it. He must like to drive with the window open, she thought, to feel the wind on his face. So did she.

"Why aren't you in Seattle?"

"Meeting ran later than I expected. Much later, in fact. Looks like I'll be here for another day. I was with a potential client and he insisted on wining and dining me. I couldn't wait to get out of there. Finally told them I had a date for tonight, and made my escape."

"Do you?" she asked.

"Do I what?"

"Have a date for tonight."

"That's what I was going to ask you. Do you like ice cream?"

"Do I *like* ice cream?" She laughed. "Do ballerinas wear toe shoes?"

His lips opened wide in a devastating smile. "Well then, hop in."

Hop in? Should she? She studied his face in the moonlight and decided he was too handsome for her own good. She'd love to go out with him. What sane woman wouldn't? But if she spent another few hours in his presence, she'd only make it harder for herself when he left the next day.

She swept a lock of gleaming hair behind one ear and gestured toward her cutoffs and T-shirt. "My outfit may be fine for the job, but I doubt if it's appropriate for a night on the town."

His eyes traveled the length of her bare legs with an appreciative glow. "As a matter of fact, I'm the one who's overdressed for the place I have in mind. As I recall, the sign outside said Shoes And Shirt Required. Didn't say a thing about long pants.''

She laughed. "I don't know, Kyle. I—"

"Come on, lady." He reached across the car and pushed open the passenger door. "Be daring. I promise you a good time."

Reason and caution deserted her. "Oh, why not." She circled the car and climbed in.

"You're the last person I expected to find on my doorstep tonight," she said after he'd backed out and gunned the sports car through her quiet neighborhood onto Beach Boulevard.

He looked at her and met her gaze briefly before turning back to the wheel. "I couldn't leave without seeing you again."

He asked about her day, probed with endless questions and seemed to be fascinated by what seemed to her the most obscure details. He said he'd spent the day in boring meetings, and the high point of his day was dinner.

"You'll never guess what I ordered," he said.

Their eyes met. "Lobster," they said in unison. Their laughter was immediate and spontaneous.

"I hope your client didn't steal it away from you."

"No. But it didn't taste the same without you there," he said, his voice low and deep.

She felt that now-familiar flutter in her stomach and had to turn her face to the window to hide the wash of affection she knew must be written there.

He drove down to Huntington Beach and parked just a few blocks down from the restaurant where they'd eaten the night before. "I saw this place last night," he said, indicating the small ice-cream parlor in front of them. "What do you say to a double cone and a walk on the beach?"

"Fantastic!" Desiree jumped out of the car and pulled on her lightweight sweater. The air felt cool and pleasant, with the sound of nearby crashing waves and the pungent salty smell of the sea.

Kyle pushed open the glass door and they stepped inside the dimly lit interior of the ice-cream parlor. A teenage girl in a white smock smiled at them as she vigorously rubbed the long glass counter with a rag. "You're just in time," she said. "I was shutting off the lights. I'm about to close up."

Kyle stepped up to the glass display case and raised an eyebrow at Desiree inquiringly. "What'll you have?"

She pondered for a moment over the vast array of different flavors, finally tapping the glass above a container of mint chocolate-chip. "I could go more exotic, but I think I'll stick to my favorite flavor tonight."

He glanced at the barrel of pale green ice cream below the glass. "Oh? Strawberry?"

She stared at him, lips parted in surprise. Strawberry? Was he kidding? "Are you color-blind?" she asked.

It was intended as a joke. The look in his eyes told her it was no laughing matter. His face reddened slightly beneath his tan and he averted his eyes, his mouth drawn into a tight line. "Why? What'd I say?"

"Nothing, it's just that . . ." She could have kicked herself. Why hadn't she been more tactful? "This flavor. It's mint chip. It's green."

"Oh." He shrugged off his embarrassment. "Yes, I'm color-blind." He turned quickly to the girl behind the counter, who was staring at them curiously. "She'll have two scoops. Mint chip. The green stuff." He ordered fresh peach, paid for the cones and guided her outside.

"I'm sorry, Kyle," she began. "I didn't—"

"Forget it." His clipped tone warned her to drop the subject. But why? She was sorry she'd embarrassed him, but color blindness shouldn't be a mournful condition. Why was he so touchy about it?

"Come on," he said, grabbing her by the arm and urging her to hurry.

His enthusiasm was contagious. She forgot everything in her sudden need to be closer to the lapping surf. They found a staircase at the end of the block and bounded down the concrete steps to the beach. They took off their shoes and left them on the bottom step. He rolled up his pant legs and she laughed, telling him he looked like a schoolboy in knickers. He threatened to capsize her ice-cream cone if she didn't behave herself.

They joined hands and raced across the wide stretch of cool gritty sand, which glowed pale gray in the moonlight. He slowed a few yards from the water's edge and they strolled along in silence. She enjoyed the feel of the wet dark sand beneath her feet and the sweet frosty taste of the ice cream.

"Isn't this great?" he grinned, squeezing her hand and swinging their arms.

"Yes." A laugh bubbled up inside her chest. "I haven't had this much fun in ages. Outside of the station, that is."

"Why not?"

"I don't know. I've worked nights for so long, my social life has been pretty nil. I get such a thrill out of my job, I end up spending a lot of time there. The special tracks I run take a lot of research and prerecording."

"Still, you've got to leave time for fun. You don't strike me as an overly serious type. In fact, from what I've read, people who are—people who create clutter—"

"Create clutter?" She punched him lightly on the arm. "How rude. Is it my fault if the maid decided to take the week off?"

"People who create clutter," he went on, his lips twitching with suppressed laughter, "are often marvelously relaxed. They're usually open to new ideas, imaginative, spontaneous. They respond to the moment. Is that true of you?"

"Sometimes." A challenging look crept into his green eyes, and she sensed he intended more by the question than appeared on the surface. "I just haven't been around very many other crazy spontaneous people lately."

"It's time we changed that," he said.

The shiver that ran through Desiree's body had nothing to do with the breeze that whipped her hair across her cheek. She pulled her sweater more tightly around her.

"Cold?" he asked.

"No. I'm fine."

"You can have my jacket if you'd like." He began to shrug out of the tailored suit jacket.

"No, thank you, that's not necessary," she said quickly, then flashed him a grin. "Anyway, it would look absurd. The sleeves would probably hang down to my knees."

"I'm not *that* tall. Only five-ten. That's less than average. Practically short."

"You seem tall to me."

He finished the last bite of his ice-cream cone. "That's only because you're such a tiny pixie yourself." When he saw her grimace at his choice of words, he stopped and slipped an arm around her waist. "Hey! What's wrong with being short?"

She almost forgot his question, she was so entranced by the feel of his strong body next to hers, the sound of his voice against her ear.

"It's a pain. I can't reach the top shelves in my kitchen let alone get to the dipstick to check the oil in my car. Clothes off the rack never fit me right. Every time I buy a pair of pants I have to cut at least six inches off at the hem. And since I'm so small it seems I've had to fight all my life to be noticed, to be respected."

He studied her a moment in silence. "You didn't have to fight to catch *my* attention," he said softly. "I think you're the perfect height."

"Perfect?" To disguise her rising discomposure, she made a face and imitated Barbara's Brooklyn accent. "You think five-feet and three-eighths is perfect?"

Chuckling, he drew her closer, both hands at her waist. "Do you have any idea what a relief it is to be out with a woman who doesn't have to worry about whether or not she'll be too tall for me if she wears heels?"

She laughed, loving his ability to put her at ease. "That's one problem I've never had, no matter who I've gone out with. And thank goodness you're not any taller. I practically have to bend my neck in half to look up at you as it is."

"At last, a woman who can appreciate my height." He leaned forward and took a large bite of her cone. "You know, except for the chocolate chips in your ice cream, the peach and mint chip look exactly the same color to me."

She searched his face, relieved at the lack of embarrassment she saw there, but unsure how to respond. The breeze had ruffled his hair and she stifled an impulse to brush the unruly strands off his forehead. "What do they look like to you?"

"Sort of a light brown. Beige, I guess. I assume they're completely different colors?"

She nodded. "Do you have trouble seeing all colors?"

"No. Mainly reds and greens."

His nearness and the mild fragrance of his cologne were doing strange things to her heartbeat. She finished her cone, stepped back and knelt in the sand a few feet away and rinsed her hands in the gently flowing surf.

A sudden thought occurred to her. Last night, he said he'd wanted to be a pilot, but that circumstances had prevented it. With a jolt of painful awareness, she remembered reading somewhere that normal color perception was mandatory for air force and commercial pilots.

She stood up and shook her hands dry. Hesitantly she asked, "That's what kept you from becoming a pilot, isn't it? Being color-blind?"

"Yes."

"Why? Why is color perception so important?"

"Warning lights, mainly. In military and commercial aircrafts, each light in the cockpit conveys a specific message. Green is status quo. Amber's a warning. Low oil pressure, that kind of thing. Red's an emergency situation. There are lights on the wing tips, too. At night the color tells you if other aircraft are approaching or heading away. And if your radio should malfunction, the tower can signal landing instructions in code with colored lights. They can't take a chance on someone who might misinterpret the signals." He let out an ironic laugh. "I passed all the other tests with ease but . . ." He shrugged.

"If that's what you really wanted to be, I'm sorry."

"Don't be. I don't regret it, not anymore." He took her hand again and continued on down the beach. "I've become successful at what I do, and it didn't keep me on the ground. I may not be able to fly for an airline or the air force, but I can still fly a private plane. I'm restricted to daytime flight, that's all."

"Really? You have a pilot's license?"

He nodded. "And a twin-engine Bonanza. I use it for pleasure outings, short trips. It's a great little machine." He gestured animatedly with one hand. "There's a special kind of excitement to flying. Up there you've got the entire sky to yourself, the world spread out beneath you. It's incredible. Have you ever been up in a private plane?''

A shudder ran through her body and she shook her head. ''No, never. And I never want to. I have enough trouble getting myself to relax on a commercial flight.''

He seemed disappointed. ''If you're inferring that light planes aren't safe, they are. It all depends on the experience of the mechanic and the pilot.''

She shrugged. ''Maybe.'' After what happened three years ago, she'd vowed never to fly in a private plane. But she didn't want to think about it now. The night was too perfect, with the crisp evening breeze, the dark velvet sky, and the frothy tide softly ebbing and flowing just a few yards away. She turned her head, focusing on the perfect sets of twin footprints they left behind in the damp sand. His looked large and solid, a protective force next to her tiny ones. She thought how wonderful it would be to have a man at her side, always, to walk with, talk with, share with. Not just any man. Kyle.

Stop it, Desiree, she thought. You know it's impossible.

She searched quickly for a new topic to divert her mind. ''What do you do about traffic lights?''

''I can tell by position. Red's always on top. Green's on the bottom.''

''Oh. I never thought of that.''

''It's only a problem when there's a flashing light. I'm never sure if it's red or yellow, so I just plow right through.''

She gasped, then saw his devilish expression and laughed. ''You seem to have adjusted well.''

''No, I haven't.'' He stopped and wrapped his arms around her, pressing her close to him. ''As you could see I'm still embarrassed about it.''

Her pulse accelerated as she looked up at him and felt her slender body warm against the hard strength of his. It seemed only natural to slide her arms around his waist. ''Why is it embarrassing?'' she asked.

''It's a flaw. It means there's something permanently wrong with me. When the leaves turn colors in autumn, I can't see them. The trees all look the same to me. Just plain dull brown.''

She hugged him tightly around the waist, wishing she had the courage to rub her hands up across his back, to learn the feel of his contoured muscles against the palms of her hands. "It hurts me to think of all the beauty you're missing," she whispered.

He tilted his head back and looked at her, his eyes reflecting the moonlight's glow. "All the beauty I'll ever need to see is right here, in my arms." He raised his hand and she felt the rough strength of his index finger caress her cheek and trace the curve of her jaw. When his fingertip reached the corner of her lips, he paused, his eyes locking with hers. She read there his admiration, his desire and his intent.

Desiree's heart seemed first to stop, then beat double time. She shouldn't kiss him. She should step back, then deliver her friends-only smile. But just as moths are drawn to flame, she boldly followed the dictates of her instinct. She stood on her tiptoes, moved her hands to the back of his neck, threaded her fingers through his short silky hair and offered her lips to him. Dazed by the fire of need blazing through her veins, she begged, "Kiss me."

He didn't need a second invitation. His mouth came down on hers in a single expedient motion, the force of his lips matching the desperation in her voice. It was a rough caress, an explosive release of pent-up emotion. His lips pressed into hers. His arms crushed her against him. She didn't mind; she welcomed it. She'd wanted this, needed this. Desiree felt like a prisoner set free, a blind person granted sight.

When at last he tore his lips from hers, they took a simultaneous ragged breath. Their eyes locked, glimmering with delight in the newness of what they'd just found. She felt his body tremble slightly against hers, as if he were struggling to contain the same impulses raging within her.

"Desiree..." he whispered.

It was the first time she'd heard him say her name. He whispered it reverently, with the throaty sensual French inflection for which it was intended. It sounded like a prayer.

When his lips met hers again, it was with gentle persuasion. His mouth moved slowly, teasingly as if savoring her warm softness. She felt her knees weaken beneath the feather-light contact, and he slid his hands tenderly up and down the length of her back, then pulled her more tightly against him. His tongue flicked back and forth across her lips, then delved into her moist mouth, hot and insistent. She arched against him, unsure if the rapid thudding she felt against his hard chest was the beating of his heart or her own.

Kyle drew his lips back slightly, then trailed fiery kisses across her cheek and buried his face in her hair at the side of her neck. He heaved an uneven sigh, still holding her against him tightly, possessively.

"You are *Desiree*. Desired. Wanted. Longed for." He pulled his head back and brought his wide firm hands up to cradle her face. "I've wanted to kiss you from the first moment I saw you, standing there like some enchanted sprite in your studio. And when I had you in my arms last night, before we said goodnight..." He paused, taking a deep breath as if to steady himself. "I could see you weren't ready, that I was going too fast. I can't tell you how hard it's been to wait, to force myself to keep my hands off you."

"You didn't have to wait long," she whispered.

"Wrong." His lips nuzzled her ear. "We met on the air, at three-forty-five yesterday afternoon. I started dreaming of you even then. That was ... let's see ..." He raised his head, eyes squinting as he made the mental calculation. "Thirty-one hours ago. Believe me, it's been long enough." He kissed her again, harder this time, then drew back and moved his eyes lingeringly over her face, as if trying to memorize every detail.

A sudden rush of icy water raced up the sand and swirled about their ankles. Desiree squealed as the wave splashed their bare legs with cold salty spray and foam. Kyle grabbed her hand, and they made a dash for higher land.

"Let's go home," he said. He said the word home as if it was his too, a place they both shared. For some reason she didn't mind. They retraced their steps to his car and drove back to her house, their feet still bare and sandy.

When they arrived she opened the car door and gestured toward the house with a nod of her head. "Come on in and get cleaned up. I'll make you a mug of Mexican coffee, my own special recipe."

"Who could refuse an invitation like that?"

They dusted off most of the sand from their feet, then went inside. His eyes widened when they passed through her sparkling-clean living room.

"Hey! What happened here in the past twenty-four hours? The maid get back from vacation?"

"Spring cleaning," she retorted, grabbing his hand and pulling him down the hall. "Out of season."

"Well, the place looks terrific."

"Don't get too excited. The back half of the house still thinks it's the dead of winter."

She tried to hurry him through her bedroom to the master bathroom. She'd forgotten about the array of clothing, books, nail polish, bottles of perfume and other paraphernalia spread in disarray across her dresser-top. He didn't appear to notice, however. He'd stopped beside her unmade bed and wrapped one hand around a carved bedpost, which reached his chin.

"You weren't kidding," he said. "You've really got one hell of a bed here."

Remembering her remark the day before about her antique headboard, she followed his line of sight. He was paying more attention to the thrown-back eyelet comforter and the exposed rumpled sheets than he was to the exquisitely carved mahogany.

She gave him a shove toward the bathroom. "You have no respect for antiques."

"I do!" he said. "I have a deep and abiding respect for antiques." He yanked back the shower curtain over the porcelain bathtub. "Now here's an antique. A pink bathtub! Where would you find a pink bathtub nowadays?"

Her mouth opened and she took a sharp breath, watching him closely. Should she tell him? The bathtub was green. She closed her mouth again.

"You're right," she said. "You hardly ever see pink anymore."

He seemed unaware of his mistake or her reaction to it, and she was glad. Quirking a brow in her direction he asked "Want to take a bath?"

"No! Not together, at least." She tried to sound irritated and failed miserably. She handed him a wash cloth and towel from the linen closet and turned on the water in the tub. "I'm going to rinse my feet off. Or do you want to go first?"

"No, please. Be my guest."

Standing alongside the tub, she dipped one foot under the running water. She bent forward, washed the sand from between her toes and turned around, switching legs. She was halfway through before she realized what a view her far-too-brief cutoffs must be providing Kyle. She jerked upright and whirled around.

"Don't mind me," he said. The warm glitter in his eyes made her cheeks flush red-hot.

"I'm done. I'll just wait for you in the other room." Desiree grabbed her towel and escaped out the door, her feet dripping water as she ran.

"This was a real treat," Kyle said, finishing the last of the coffee she'd laced with tequila and a generous helping of cream. She sat beside him on the living-room couch, her bare feet, now clean and dry, tucked beneath her.

"Guess you don't see Mexican coffee too often up in Seattle," she said. "A definite drawback to being a northerner."

He caught her gaze. "There are other drawbacks I can think of. Much more disturbing ones." Putting down his cup, he drew her into his arms, his lips against her hair. "I had a great time tonight."

"So did I."

He held her against him for a moment, then bent his head and pressed his lips lightly against hers. He smoothed her cheek with his fingertips and kissed her again, and again, lingering longer with each soft touch of his mouth on hers.

A cloud of desire enveloped her, wrapping her in its swirling depths. She wanted to give in to her body's yearning, to press herself against his hard strength and let his body imbue her with warmth. Instead, she gripped his shoulders lightly and whispered his name against his lips. "Wait," she said. "We should—"

"Should what?"

"Say good-night. I mean goodbye. You're going home to-morrow, and—"

"Am I?" He brushed his lips against hers. "That depends on you."

"On me?"

He nodded, drawing back slightly. "As I said before, I'll be tied up in a meeting all day tomorrow, but I'm in no rush to fly home. We've got Friday night and the whole weekend ahead of us. If you'll let me see you again...if you want me to stay...I'll be here until the last possible second, until Monday morning at dawn." He searched her face for an answer. "Do you want me to stay?"

He took advantage of her moment of hesitation to lower his mouth to hers, his kiss kindling a fire that burst into flame deep within her. His hands roved across her shoulders, then tenderly massaged her back before sliding around to brush the sides of her breasts. His mouth moved slowly, softly against hers, coaxing her lips apart until he was able to taste the honeyed recesses within.

She tried to resist. She couldn't. Melting against him, she lifted her arms to caress his neck, her fingertips lacing through the thick short waves of his hair. His tongue circled hers, explored, dipped deeper, deeper, as if searching for each hidden sweet taste.

He turned, lowering her gently onto the sofa. His hand caressed first one soft rounded breast and then the other through the thin fabric of her shirt. A thousand tiny explosions coursed through her, like sudden gunfire. Her entire body began to throb with sexual awareness, from her breasts, so full and aching, to an exquisite hot wetness between her thighs.

A moan escaped her lips. He lowered his body on top of hers and recaptured her mouth in a deep burning kiss. She felt the evidence of his arousal, hard and insistent against her. It only intensified her desire. Make love to me, her body sang out at the same time as her mind shouted, No! With the last vestige of her self-control, she tore her mouth from his.

"Kyle, wait," she gasped. "This is . . . it's all happening so fast. I haven't known you long enough. I—"

"I feel as if I've known you all my life," he said huskily. His palm caressed her cheek, gently urging her to meet his warm gaze. This time there was another, more immediate meaning in the question he whispered feverishly in her ear.

"Do you want me to stay?"

Five

N-no!'' Desiree pulled herself out of his arms and jumped to her feet. Her fingers trembled as they fumbled to straighten her T-shirt over her breasts.

Kyle sat up on the couch and leaned forward, resting his forearms on his thighs, hands clasped together. For a while he stared at the plush Persian area rug beneath his feet, taking slow, deep breaths, as if struggling to regain his composure. His words, when he spoke, sounded clipped, yet still congenial. ''Do you mean *no*, you don't want me to stay the weekend, or *no*, you don't want me to spend the night?''

Desiree turned toward the fireplace and stared at the dark lifeless hearth, her fingers tightly interlaced to stop them from shaking. What was she doing? What had come over her? She'd wanted to go out with Kyle, there was no denying it, but she'd promised herself not to get involved with him. How could she have let things get so out of hand?

''No . . . to both questions,'' she said, her voice tremulous.

His head whipped up. ''What?''

She faced him again. "There's no need for you to change your plans to go back to Seattle. I won't be able to see you tomorrow."

His forehead furrowed in a puzzled frown. "Why not? Don't you get off at six?"

"No. I mean yes. But I'll have to work late."

"How late?"

"It . . . depends. There's a bunch of commercials I have to produce. It might take hours. I've got to put music behind them, do the vocals, cut them onto tape, record them on cart—"

"Cart?"

"Short for cartridge, like an eight-track. Makes it simple to pop into the deck. I should have done it tonight, but—"

"Okay," he conceded. "You're busy tomorrow night. What about Saturday?"

She shook her head. "I have to work all day. All weekend, in fact."

"All weekend?" He stared at her, incredulous. "What kind of a schedule is that? You must get off sometime?"

"I . . . don't know," she said evasively. "I just got this new shift. The schedule's not final yet."

He stood up, shoved his hands in his pockets, the muscles in his tanned forearms rigid and distended. "I see."

Guiltily, she lowered her gaze. Her hands wanted to touch his cheek, his neck, his arm. Her lips yearned for the feel of his mouth on hers again, the taste of his tongue encircling hers. But she knew if he took her in his arms again, if she gave herself up to the thrill of his tantalizing caresses, all her willpower would fly out the window. He'd end up spending the night. She knew once she'd made love to Kyle, her heart would never be able to let him go.

She took several steps back. An unpleasant shiver ran up her legs as her bare feet left the cozy warmth of the area rug and came in contact with the cold hardwood floor. "Th-thank you for the walk on the beach, Kyle. It was . . . wonderful. And thank you again for the roses. I—"

"Desiree." The deep resonant timbre in his voice made her jump. "I'm not leaving this house until you tell me when I can see you again."

"You can't."

"Look, if you're busy this weekend, I understand. I'll call you when I get home. We'll pick a weekend, sometime next month. I'll fly back down."

"No!" Her back struck the credenza and she froze as he took a step toward her. "It's no use, Kyle. I . . . I'm glad I met you. But . . ." She lowered her eyes. "I can't get involved with you . . . with anyone."

"The hell you can't!" He crossed the room in two strides, grabbed her firmly by the shoulders and turned her to face him. "We're already involved, dammit!"

"No, we're not. We can't be. You live too far away. It's—" Her voice broke and she turned her head to avoid his angry gaze. "It's wrong for me. For both of us."

"Wrong? How can it be wrong? Desiree, there's something special between us. I felt it the moment I saw you and I'm certain of it now. We were meant to be together." One arm swept down to the small of her back and the other cradled her neck, imprisoning her against his hard chest as he lowered his face to hers. She stiffened, struggling to maintain her resolve despite the warm glow of desire that rekindled within her body each time it came into contact with his.

"I felt you respond to me," he said. "I feel you responding now. You want me as much as I want you. Admit it!"

She squeezed her eyes shut and shook her head, trying to block out the fiery eyes and sensuous lips so dangerously close to her own. A small sob escaped her throat and she blinked back tears. "No, Kyle! I—"

He cut off her words with the pressure of his lips. His hands gripped her head and back tightly, allowing no resistance. His lips ravished hers with a bruising force, moving back and forth, round and round. His hand traveled across her back, up and down her spine, sending rockets of desire shuttling to uncharted regions of her body. His tongue darted between her lips, across her teeth, then delved into her moist mouth. He consumed her with an impassioned hunger, his heart beating against hers in a wild polyphony of frantic need.

Desiree's mind reeled. The throbbing in her chest spread down toward her loins, where it pulsed a frenzied rhythm. The tiny part of her that could still think told her to break away from his embrace. But her body, out of control, acted of its own volition. Her arms wrapped around his back. Her fingers grasped his shoulder blades, pulling him closer. She molded her body against his lean muscled frame.

At her response he moaned, low and deep in his throat. Apparently sensing she'd resist no further, he relaxed his hold and pulled back slightly. She felt an instant of disappointment, thinking he was going to let her go. But before she could open her eyes, he took a ragged breath and began to move his lips slowly, gently, persuasively over hers. His fingertips stroked through the silky hair at her nape. His warm sweet breath fanned her mouth as his feathery kisses tickled and teased her lips, then brushed across her cheeks, nose and jaw.

She felt her limbs melt like candle wax against a flame as he again lowered his mouth to drop a series of long sensuous kisses along her neck and throat. Her breathing was short and shallow and she leaned her head back to allow him full access to her throat. She held him tighter, no longer certain her quaking legs could support her weight.

Ever so slowly he kissed his way back up her neck, across her cheek to her forehead. Then, tenderly, he folded her in his arms and brought her head down against his chest.

"You see how it is, Desiree," he said softly, his lips moving against her hair.

Even if she had wanted to push herself away from him, there wasn't strength left in her limbs. Her cheek lay against the softness of his shirt, and she could feel his chest, moving up and down in an erratic rhythm against hers as they caught their breath.

He was right; there was no denying the attraction she felt for him, and it seemed that he felt the same way. But what exactly did he want from her? A weekend fling? Someone to keep his bed warm on his business trips down south? Or did he imagine there could be more to it than that?

She knew, in her heart, that any kind of future between them was out of the question. His home, his work was in Seattle, and hers was here, more than a thousand miles away. She knew what it was like to be separated from the one you loved. She'd never forget the loneliness of those long months without Steve, longing for his company at the end of each day, reaching out for him in the empty darkness at night. Was what happened his fault? Or was it hers? She still wasn't certain. But no matter who was to blame, she'd learned her lesson. If she wanted a career in radio, she had to remain free and independent. She couldn't give her heart to any man.

"Kyle," she said, tilting her head back and fingering the lapel of his shirt as she looked up at him, "I can't hide the way I feel about you. But there's no way a relationship can work between us. I tried to tell you last night. My job—"

"I heard what you said last night. Every word. Your lack of job security, the way you have to move every few years, all the excuses you've learned to cling to as reasons not to get involved with anyone. So you might get fired any minute, so what? We already live a thousand miles apart. What difference would another few miles make?"

All the difference in the world, she wanted to say. But she didn't want to dredge up the painful memories she'd managed to bury so deep inside her. Still, somehow she had to make him see.

"One of us will end up getting hurt," she whispered. "I know it. I—"

"No. You can't know that." He kissed her again, long and hard. "I'm not trying to predict how things will end up between us, Desiree. But if it's meant to be, it will be. Let's just take things one day at a time. I've waited a long time to find you, and I'm not about to give you up now."

A bird chirped outside Desiree's window. She opened her eyes, startled, and squinted against the first faint light of a gray dawn. She must have finally dozed off. How many hours did she toss and turn, thoughts of Kyle and his impassioned caresses burning into her mind?

After he left last night, she'd had to lean against the credenza for support, her legs as limp as a rag doll's. It was a long while before she found the strength to stumble down the hall to her bedroom, even longer before she finally undressed and lay on the bed.

Now, many sleepless hours later, her mind still spun with confusion. Why wouldn't he listen to her? Why did he insist that he'd see her again? Why did that make her feel like shouting for joy?

It didn't seem possible they'd only met two days before. Nothing seemed the same. Her room, cast in shadows by the unfamiliar early-morning light, looked foreign to her. Her bed, which always seemed so warm and inviting beneath the fluffy white eyelet comforter, had never felt so hard . . . so cold . . . so empty.

Her response to Kyle's embrace filled her with equal measures of fear and exhilaration. No man's touch had ever inspired in her such fierce desire. No man. Ever. And it was more than just a physical response. She loved being with him, loved the sound of his voice, the knack he had of putting her at ease, the way he laughed at her jokes. In only two days he'd made her feel more beautiful, more feminine and desirable than she'd ever felt in her life. With the slightest encouragement, she could easily fall in love with him. And to do that would spell disaster.

What on earth was she going to do?

She threw back the covers and climbed out of bed. She went into the bathroom and pulled her nightgown over her head then stepped beneath the shower's warm stinging spray. He'd left without saying if he'd call or stop by. She'd told him she'd be busy all weekend, so presumably he'd return to Seattle tonight. Or would he?

The morning sped past as she straightened up her bedroom and den, paid a few bills and watered the flower beds in her front yard. She showed up at the station with an hour to spare, produced three commercials in record time and slipped into her seat at the console at precisely two o'clock. She was more than halfway through her shift and was standing by her counter logging promos when Barbara threw open the door.

"Hi, Des. What's new with my—" Barbara pulled to an abrupt halt in the doorway and stared at Desiree, her eyes wide. "What is that you're wearing?"

Desiree shot an impatient glance over her shoulder. "It's quite obvious what I'm wearing."

"But it's . . . it's a *skirt*!" She uttered the word in disbelief, as if a skirt was the last thing on earth a petite thirty-year-old female would wear.

Desiree smoothed out the swirling folds of the floral wraparound and fluffed the ruffled V-neckline of her soft turquoise blouse. She bought the outfit months ago, on impulse, even though she had nowhere special to wear it. "I realize it's a skirt," she said testily.

"What's the occasion? Come on, tell me!" Barbara cried. "For two years you've never worn anything but cutoffs or jeans. You must be going somewhere!" Her glance darted to the vase of roses which still graced the counter beside the console. "Ahh! The Hunk Returns, is that it? And you *do* like him!" She giggled loudly and placed a candy bar on the counter. "Far be it from me to say I told you so." She flounced out the door.

A moment later Tom poked his head inside. "My God," he said. "It's true. You are wearing a skirt."

"Get lost!" Desiree cried, glaring at him.

Tom shook his head. "What a woman. For two years I've offered my body on a plate, and who does she fall for? Some guy in a rented Maserati."

"Oh, get out of here!" Desiree picked up a paperback and hurled it at him. The door slammed just in time.

She climbed up on the stool, put on her headphones and drummed her fingernails against the console, waiting for her cue.

"102 FM, KICK on this Friday afternoon," she said into the mike. "That was Kenny Rogers with 'Why Was I So Blind?' from his latest album 'Cutting Loose.' The weekend's almost on us now and we'll all be cutting loose! It's ten minutes before five o'clock."

She played three more songs, then ran a commercial break. She began to read a public service announcement about an annual aerobics dance for the National Heart Association when she heard the studio door open again. She froze, not daring to look over her shoulder. *No one* would come in while she was on the air. No one except . . .

"You can win some exciting prizes," she said, trying to keep her voice steady as she read, "get some great exercise and have a whole lot of fun." She heard the door shut.

"Sign up now. That's The Dance for Heart . . ."

Strong hands came to rest on her shoulder blades. Warm lips pressed against her neck. She stifled a gasp as a frenzied shiver traveled up her spine.

" . . . at the Anaheim Convention Center . . ."

She felt his hands rove up and down her bare arms, his body press against her back. A heady languor descended over her, as if her veins were flowing with thick sweet syrup. Her voice slowed and deepened with each touch of his fingers.

" . . . next Saturday, June twenty-seventh." Her chest rose and fell with increasing rapidity as his mouth nuzzled against her throat. Her ears began to pound. She strained to hear her own voice.

"For registration forms, call the National Heart Association at 555-3110, or stop by the studio here at KICK."

She flicked off the mike and punched a button on the cart deck to start the next song. Pulling off her headphones, she heaved a sigh of relief. He crossed his arms underneath her breasts and pulled her back against his hard frame.

"I missed you," he said against her ear, his voice soft and deep.

"Don't you know what a red warning light is?" She tried to sound indignant, but the words came out like a soft sigh.

"Yes," he murmured. "It's the signal that flashes in my brain every time I see you."

She leaned her head against his shoulder and closed her eyes, enveloped by his warmth and the spicy scent of his cologne. "I'm talking about the big red beacon on the wall outside the control-room door," she said.

He lifted his head. "Red? You mean that green light telling me it's all right to come in?"

She gasped, remembering he was color-blind. "Oh! You thought it was green?" But when she pulled out of his embrace to look at him she saw a flash of devilment in his eyes. "Liar!"

He laughed. "I assumed it was red. I know what a warning light means."

"Then why did you—"

"I like to surprise you. Catch you when your back's turned, so to speak. Far more exciting."

"Well," she huffed, "you'll have to stop doing it. The mike picks up every little sound."

He leaned over and breathed close to her ear. "Every little sound?"

"Yes."

"Would it pick up this sound?" He wrapped his arms around her again and kissed the side of her neck.

Her head tilted upward, as if obeying a silent command.

"Yes," she said huskily.

"And this?" He dropped kisses around the graceful curve of her neck to the hollow of her throat.

"Yes... Definitely."

"Then I guess I'll have to restrain myself while we're in here."

"I guess so." She sighed. "Otherwise I might make a mistake. Say the wrong thing. Sound...awful."

"*Au contraire*. I'll wager you've never sounded more sultry or sensuous in your life than you did on the air just now." His arms tightened around her from behind. "I only helped promote your image."

"I've been doing just fine on my own, thank you." She knew she was playing with fire. This time her job, not just her emotions, were on the line. Anyone might walk by and see them through the high windows above the console. If Sam caught them kissing, or if she missed so much as one precious cue, his rage would be immediate and intense.

She squirmed out of his arms and slipped off the stool. "I assume you missed your flight to Seattle?"

"Looks that way. Pity, isn't it?" He leaned back against the counter and crossed his arms, his eyes sliding the length of her slim figure. He whistled. "Don't you look nice tonight. Quite a change from your previous outfit."

Her cheeks grew hot. "I felt like dressing up today."

"Just in case I decided to stop by?"

"No!" She pushed him out of her way. "Because I felt like it." With a glance at the rotation chart, she cued up the next few songs.

He laughed. "Whatever the reason, I'm glad you did. I figured we'd need time for you to go home and change, but now we can fit in dinner before the show if we leave right at six."

"Dinner?" Her glance fell on his wrists, where square gold cuff links glimmered in the cuffs of his long-sleeved dress shirt. He wore the camel-brown suit she remembered from the night they met, this time with a matching vest. "Show?" she asked.

He pulled two tickets out of his breast pocket for a hit musical and handed them to her. "I had a hell of a time getting these."

She stared at the tickets in astonishment. "I've been dying to see this show but it's been sold out for months!"

"So they told me. I badgered them so long at the box office, though, they finally managed to find something. Damn good seats, too."

"When did you find time to get tickets? I thought you had a meeting today."

"I did. Things wrapped up early," he said. "I hope you didn't mean what you said last night . . . about working late?"

She opened his jacket and put them in his pocket. "Nothing could keep me here tonight if you have tickets like these."

The song on the air ended with a cold fade. She expertly segued into the next tune, then sat back on her stool.

Kyle's eyes darted about the room, finally coming to rest on the row of knobs, meters and buttons on her console. "Correct me if I'm wrong, but this equipment isn't exactly state of the art, is it?"

She shook her head and touched a hand to one of the black knobs. "No. Most control boards today have levers instead of pots like these."

"Pots?"

"Short for potentiometer. Controls the level of modulation. There usually are remote starts right in a row, so the operator doesn't have to go through as many motions." She smiled rue-fully. "Lucky me. With all the modern equipment around to-day, I end up at a station with a practically ancient system."

"But this is a major market." He leaned back against the counter, his hands in his pockets. "From what I've read you're a highly rated station in Orange County. Why doesn't the owner modernize?"

"This place is only a hobby for him. He owns several other companies that keep him busy, and he has some pretty definite ideas about what to spend his money on. The equipment works, he says. As long as we have an engineer who knows how to keep it running, he'll make it last for ages." She shrugged. "He'd rather spend his money on an airwatch pilot, if you can be-lieve that."

"An airwatch pilot? You mean you have your own man in a plane up there?"

She nodded. "I'll show you. Traffic is next. Hang on."

She whipped on her headphones and turned up the volume inside the studio for Kyle's benefit, then switched on the mike. "It's five o'clock. You've got Desiree, and this is KICK-FM, Anaheim. Now let's hear from our daredevil in the skies, Deadly Dave Dawson." She punched a button marked Traffic on the control board. "Dave?"

"Hi, Desiree. Hey, you were breathing pretty hard a few minutes ago. Who've you got in there with you? Robert Red-ford?"

She felt a blush start in her cheeks and spread to the roots of her hair. This was their typical daily banter; Dave was always kidding her about the sensual quality of her voice. How was he to know that this time his comment hit the nail on the head?

"No, not today." She tried to sound breezy. "Bob called and said he couldn't make it."

"Well, it sure sounds like you've got somebody in there."

"The truth is, Dave, I do have somebody in here." She turned and met Kyle's amused gaze. "He's a top name in his field, incredibly rich. He's devilishly handsome, has a fantas-tic body and the most gorgeous eyes you've ever seen. Care to take a guess?"

"Ahh...let's see. What color hair?"

"Sort of a... burnished mahogany."

"Aha! Tom Selleck!"

"Close. Very close. But let's just keep this our little secret, okay?" Out of the corner of her eye, she saw the buttons light up on her phone. Don't miss a trick, do they? she thought with a grin. "Now what about that traffic? How's it look out there?"

A chuckle traveled the airwaves. "Things aren't looking too bad, actually, for a Friday night. The Golden State southbound is slow and go at..."

As Dave continued the report, her earphones were plucked from her head and an arm stole around her again from behind. Quickly she flipped off the mike.

"Devilishly handsome?" he murmured, his lips against her ear. "Fantastic body? Gorgeous eyes?"

"Well, I guess I did get a little carried away." Her lips began to tremble as she sat on the stool, his hard chest pressed against her back. She couldn't stop her eyes from closing, her neck from arching back and resting against his shoulder. "As long as they think someone's in here, let's give them something to worry about."

"Great idea." He slowly rotated the stool until her side rested against him. Cupping her chin in his hand, he turned her mouth up to his and tantalized it with light soft kisses. His free hand roamed to her opposite hip, holding her captive against his chest as his tongue traced her lips, then slipped inside her mouth. She returned the kiss as it became deeper, matched fire with fire, locked her hands behind his neck and pulled him closer against her. In the back of her mind she heard a voice, distorted words, droning on in what seemed a foreign language.

"Stalled vehicle... 605 northbound... no other problems..."

She felt Kyle's hand drift down her arm, brush the side of her breast. She was spinning, as if from lack of oxygen, as if he was drawing the breath from her body.

"That's about it for..." The voice hazily penetrated her dazed state. The words formed a familiar pattern, then began to flash in her brain like a neon sign. "...Dawson, for KICK. Have a nice weekend."

She bolted upright, pushed Kyle away with a shaky hand and turned to the console, turning up the volume control. Her heart pounded in her ears as, with several instinctive expedient motions, she started the next tune and sank back against the counter, arms hanging limply at her sides. She glanced quickly out the control-room window in both directions. There was no one in sight. She blew out a sigh of relief and closed her eyes. "How do you expect me to do my job? You know I can't concentrate when you... when you—"

She glared at him. "When you hold me and... and kiss me like that!"

He lifted his palms, shrugging innocently. "Sorry."

"Keep your hands to yourself until I'm finished. All right?"

"Fine."

"Otherwise you can just sit out in the waiting area."

"I won't even get near you." They faced each other for a silent moment. Then he took one long stride toward her, like metal drawn to a magnet. "I won't touch you." One hand slid forward and grasped her waist. The other grazed her chin. "I won't hold you."

She tilted her lips up to his. She felt weak, dizzy. If he doesn't kiss me, I'll die.

He pulled her gently against him. "I won't...kiss you."

And then, to her joy and relief, he did.

Desiree relaxed against the contoured leather seat of the Maserati and closed her eyes. The engine hummed a soft lullaby, blending harmoniously with the colorful kaleidoscope of images floating through her mind.

"I didn't think anyone could tap-dance so fast," she murmured.

"Neither did I," Kyle said, chuckling. "What a show."

She couldn't remember ever spending a more enjoyable evening. They'd feasted on a delectable *canard à l'orange*—duck with orange sauce—at a small French restaurant near the theater. Kyle had ordered everything in advance, from the escargots, which Desiree had found surprisingly delicious, to the apple tart for dessert. He'd arranged for the five-course meal to be served with a minimum of delay, and they'd arrived at the Music Center just minutes before the show began.

The musical was an extravaganza of dazzling costumes and breathtaking production numbers. But even the star's spectacular toe-tapping could not compare with the thrill and pride she felt just being in Kyle's company. In his three-piece suit and silk tie, his hair carefully groomed, his face recently shaved, he looked handsome, sophisticated and indisputably masculine.

The mind-stealing embraces they'd shared in the studio, made all the more exciting by their illicit nature, never strayed from her thoughts. When his hand reached over to gently warm her thigh through the thin fabric of her skirt, it required rigorous self-control to keep her breathing steady and focus on the stage. But now, although he sat just inches from her in the cozy interior of the small sports car and his hand brushed her cheek tenderly, she felt too relaxed and content to be aroused.

"I couldn't believe it when he tapped his way up and down that staircase," he said. "And all those 360-degree turns along the way! How many stairs do you think there were?"

She shrugged drowsily and caressed his hand between her cheek and shoulder. "I don't know. Maybe fifty. Or a hundred. I think I once saw something like it in a movie, but I'm not sure." She opened her eyes and smiled. "Thank you for getting the tickets."

He squeezed her shoulder. "Anytime."

They drove along in contented silence. The effects of Desiree's sleepless night and hectic day finally caught up with her, and she drifted off to sleep. It seemed only minutes later that she heard the engine clicking off and the car's final shudder into silent stillness.

She tried to open her eyes. She felt disoriented. She tried to speak, but only managed a small drowsy yawn. All at once she felt herself being gathered up by a pair of strong arms as warm lips pressed against hers.

"Wake up, sleepyhead," he whispered. "We're home."

"Already?" She slowly opened her eyes. Moonlight splashed through the windshield, making her squint. The silvery beam that illuminated her face only touched the side of his cheek, emphasizing its smooth angular planes.

"You've been asleep for half an hour." He leaned back slightly and threaded his fingers through the hair at her nape. "Did anyone ever tell you you're beautiful when you're asleep? Even more beautiful than when you're awake, if that's possible."

"You're just saying that because it's true," she mumbled.

He laughed. "Still sharp as a tack even when you're only half-awake." He tightened his hold on her again and gazed down at her, his eyes inky-black in the darkness. "I'll have to stay on my toes to keep up with you."

His nearness, his warmth, his unique masculine scent enveloped her senses. Kiss me again, she wanted to plead. But as she lifted her hand to touch his cheek, a sudden inexplicable shyness came over her. She found herself trembling with anticipation, like a schoolgirl about to receive her first kiss. She lowered her eyes, let her hand fall away from his cheek and toyed with the edge of her smooth leather seat. "Since when did rental car companies start using Maseratis?"

"Most don't." He leaned closer. With measured slowness his thumb traced small sensuous circles at the side of her neck.

She caught her breath. Could he feel the erratic pulse beating beneath the pad of his thumb? "Where does one rent a Maserati, then?"

"There's a place near the airport." His lips hovered over hers. "They have every car you can imagine. Rolls-Royce. Mercedes. Ferrari. You name it, they've got it."

"What about . . . a Cadillac limousine?"

"Of course. One of every size and color." His breath fanned her lips. "Limos are their mainstay."

"I've always wanted to ride in a limo. An incredibly long plush limo, with a built-in bar and a TV."

"We'll have to arrange it sometime."

His lips pressed tenderly against hers, infusing her body with warmth. His tongue persuaded her lips apart, then probed her mouth, performing an intimate mating dance with her tongue. As his hands scaled her back, she locked her arms behind his neck, twisted her hands in his hair. She felt a thread of trust weave between them, through them, around them, as if entwining them in each other's arms for eternity.

"Desiree, you taste so sweet...."

His hand traced up her side to lightly graze the side of her breast, and her head fell back. A sigh of ecstasy echoed in the night as his lips moved slowly, sensuously up her throat, then covered her mouth once more.

Suddenly he winced sharply and she felt him draw back.

"What's wrong?" she asked breathlessly.

"I think the stick shift's permanently embedded in my side," he whispered.

"Oh! I'm sorry. I didn't—"

"And the windshield's all fogged up."

She giggled softly. No more than my brain, she thought. "I guess there's no point in kissing out in the car, is there?" she pointed out reasonably. "Would you like to...to come in for a brandy?"

He leaned his forehead against hers and smiled into her eyes. "I thought you'd never ask."

Six

Desiree opened the door in her credenza where she kept her liquor and poured two snifters of brandy. She watched Kyle take off his finely tailored suit jacket and hang it neatly over the back of a wing chair. His tie joined the jacket, and he opened the top two buttons of his shirt. When he apparently decided to go no further, she blew out a small sigh of relief.

"There, that's a whole lot better." He exhaled deeply and sank back into the couch. "Ever try to kiss a woman with a tie digging into your neck?"

Desiree laughed. "Not recently." She handed Kyle his drink.

"Thanks." He raised the glass in a toast. "To the most beautiful deejay I've ever met."

She sat next to him on the couch and clinked her glass against his. "That doesn't sound like much of a toast to me. How many deejays have you met?"

His lips tilted up in a roguish grin. "Not too many."

"That's what I thought. Thanks a lot."

He extended an arm across the back of the couch and turned toward her. His eyes caressed her face as he slowly sipped his brandy. "Desiree—" his voice dropped to a husky whisper "—you're one of the most beautiful women I've ever known."

Her heart hammered in her chest as she drank in his frankly adoring gaze for a long heady moment. She'd been told she was beautiful before. She'd never believed it. Hearing the words on his lips made her truly *feel* beautiful for the first time in her life. Her heart soared. She wanted to respond in kind, tell him how attractive she found him, but she couldn't find the words.

"In that case you must not have known many women," she said with a small laugh.

"Yes, I have." His eyes never wavered from hers. "But none that counted. Until now." He set down his brandy and tenderly traced the outline of her shell-like ear with a fingertip.

"Desiree, you told me you were married once," he said softly. "Will you tell me about it? What happened?"

Tearing her eyes from his gaze, she stared into the swirling amber liquid in her glass. "I'd . . . rather not talk about it."

"Why?"

"It's not a pleasant memory. It was over five years ago, but I still have scars. I'd just rather not drag it out again."

He took the glass from her hand and set it on the coffee table. The arm behind her dropped to her shoulders and his other hand cupped her face, tilting it gently up to his. "Did he hurt you?" His jaw tensed. "Because if he did—"

"No! Not in the way you mean." Held captive against his chest, she placed her hands on his waist for balance. "The scars I mentioned were purely emotional. I . . . I don't blame him for wanting the divorce. It wasn't entirely his fault. Mostly it was mine."

"I doubt that. He'd have to be a fool to give you up. A fool!"

His lips molded onto hers, possessive and gentle at the same time. His tongue thrust deeply into her mouth. His arms wrapped around her like bands of iron as he kissed her, first fiercely, then tenderly, adoringly. Her arms encircled his back as she arched against him, clutched at his hair, joined in a sweet insistent battle with his tongue. She relished the flavor of him, the heat of his skin at his nape, the silken texture of his hair. When at long last he tore his lips from hers to kiss her cheek, her nose, her forehead, the tip of her ear, she sighed with pleasure at his touch.

"Desiree, do you have any idea what you do to me?" His lips nibbled the length of her throat, then took small, teasing bites from her earlobe. "All night, I've been dying to hold you...kiss you...touch you like this."

His mouth clamped down on hers again as his hand closed over the round fullness of her breast. Slowly he rotated his fingers and palm until her desire bubbled within his grasp. His other hand pulled her blouse loose from the waistband of her skirt and slid up her back. His hand felt rough, masculine against her smooth bare flesh, sending tingles up her spine. Slowly he stood up, pulling her with him, and held her against his chest.

His hand glided down her back, slipped under her waistband, slipped even further, to cup the soft swell of her buttocks. He pressed her body against his, making her aware of the throbbing hardness of his desire, and she gasped. Even through the layers of their clothing she could feel the rapid drumming of his heart, which beat in cadence with her own.

He bent his head and captured her mouth. "You told me last night you didn't want to see me again, that you didn't want me," he whispered against her lips. "Did you mean it? Was it true?"

He met her gaze, his eyes shining with affection, alive with need. A voice inside her cried, Lie! Say yes, it's true! Her hands dug into his waist. She shook her head fiercely. "No! It wasn't true."

Without another word he swept her up into his strong muscular arms. She felt his mouth against her forehead, her cheek, the top of her head. His footsteps echoed on the hardwood floor as he carried her down the dark hallway. Oh God, she thought helplessly as she wrapped her arms around his back and buried her face against his neck. This shouldn't be happening. Not now. Not ever....

He nudged open the door to her bedroom with his foot and strode inside, lowering her gently onto her double bed. She heard him fumble with the bedside lamp, then a flick of the switch and the room was filled with soft golden light. As if in a dream, she watched him shrug out of his vest and toss it onto a nearby chair, then sit down on the edge of the bed and take off his shoes.

Stop! her conscience warned. Before it's too late. Still wearing his shirt and pants, he turned toward her and grasped her foot, pulling off first one sandal and then the other. He cradled her foot in his hands, massaged the high arch, circled his thumb over her toes.

"Such tiny feet," he said with wonder. "So petite. So delicate. And your legs...beautiful. Perfect shape." His hand slid up one bare calf, under her skirt to cup her knee. She wasn't wearing stockings; she never did in summer. His touch sent flames licking up her thighs.

Don't do this, said a voice inside her head. You'll be sorry. She pulled herself upright on the bed, her body stiff with uncertainty, her pulse racing.

"Kyle, wait."

"Why? Why should we wait?" He pulled her down on the bed next to him, held her against the length of his warm body. "You know how I feel about you. I've made no secret of it." His voice dropped to a husky whisper. "Am I reading something that isn't there? Or do you feel the same way about me?"

"You know I do," she whispered.

"Then let me show you how much I care. Let me make love to you."

"We shouldn't. It's not right for me. For us. It's too soon."

"I know things are happening fast between us. I never imagined it could be this way. But that doesn't mean it's not right." His hands stroked her cheeks as he gazed lovingly into her eyes. "Desiree, there's nothing more beautiful than what we feel for each other right now."

Right now. His words drummed in her head, bringing to the surface all her reservations, all her fears. Right now. For the moment. Temporary. Temporary insanity.

"No, Kyle!" She shook her head and tried to roll away from him on the bed, but only got as far as her back. He took hold of her arms and raised himself above her on his elbows. One hard thigh nestled between her legs and held her fast.

"Why?" he whispered. "Tell me. Help me to understand. What are you afraid of?"

Of you. Of me. That I'll learn to need you. That I'll fall in love with you and never recover. She couldn't make love to a man without giving her heart, her soul, and she was already perilously close to giving both to Kyle. Monday morning you'll be gone, she thought, and I'll be left empty and aching.

She wanted to tell him, to try to explain, but her throat felt so constricted she couldn't speak.

"You said the other night that you'll never get married again, that your divorce was inevitable. Don't you think you're being a little hard on yourself? Are you so afraid of failure that you won't allow yourself to love anyone again?"

She closed her eyes. "I don't know . . . yes," she managed in a low quiver. "That's . . . part of it."

"Have you been with anyone since then?" he asked softly.

She shook her head. Unbidden tears sprang into her eyes.

He smoothed her hair back and kissed away her tears. "Don't be afraid, Desiree. We can never be certain what the future holds for us. But don't let that stop you from living, from loving."

The tears brimmed over and trickled down her cheeks.

"Don't cry, my darling. Don't cry." His lips moved across her eyes, cheeks and chin and brushed away her tears, absorbing them into his own mouth. "Oh, God, Desiree, I'm sorry."

He lay on his side and cuddled her close against him for a time, massaging her back and heaving long steadying breaths as if fighting to regain control over his body. Finally, his voice deep and vibrant, he said, "I didn't mean to push you into something you're not ready for. I'm sorry. I don't want to hurt you, my darling. I only want to love you."

My darling. A shuddering sigh escaped her control as he covered her forehead with languorous kisses. No one had ever called her my darling. No one. Not even Steve. Until this moment she didn't realize how much she'd always longed to hear just those words, in just the way he said them.

Her arms looped around his back. Her hands tangled in his hair. Oh, Kyle. I didn't want to need you. I didn't want to want you. But I do. Her eyes met his with a wordless plea and she tilted her lips up to his.

With a low moan he rolled on top of her. His lips touched hers again, with such sensitivity and gentle adoration it took her breath away. His tongue slid between her lips, then encircled hers with a slow tender intimacy. The kiss went on and on as his hands roamed over her shoulders, then down to caress her breasts through her silky blouse.

She felt herself relax beneath him. All her reasons to resist began to drift away, one by one, to some dark forgotten corner of her mind. It's going to be all right...somehow he'll make it right... His hand reached down to unbutton her blouse, and when he reached inside her lacy bra to cup her breast, a shudder of pleasure rocketed through her and she called his name out loud. He raised her up slowly and slid the blouse and wispy bra from her body. At his sharp intake of breath she felt her heart begin to pound.

"You're so beautiful," he said huskily. He laid her back down and kissed her lightly as his hand covered one throbbing naked breast. His fingers stroked gently, seeking only to please. With slow circular motions he kneaded the rose-colored nipple until it sprang to life beneath his thumb. His touch sent tiny jolts of electricity through her, like sparks on a live wire. Soft moans of desire escaped her throat.

Her hands roamed across his back, then tugged feverishly at his shirt until it pulled free of his waistband. She ran exploring fingers along the bare smooth skin above his waist, traced the hard distinct ridge in the center of his back.

"I want to see you," she whispered. "I want to feel your chest against mine." With quivering fingers she reached around to grasp the placket of his shirt.

"Here, let me help you," he chuckled softly. He sat up and quickly removed the unwanted barrier between them and let it drop to the floor.

His chest was even more magnificent than she'd imagined. Dark curly hair covered the taut contours of his upper pectorals, then descended in crisp swirls down the center to a thin tapering line that disappeared into his pants. She lifted hesitant fingers to his smooth, lightly-tanned skin, then plowed through

his soft chest hair. She sensed a barely leashed passion burning beneath the surface of his skin, and it matched the fire raging beneath her own.

He slid down on the bed and enclosed the pink pointed crown
of one breast in his mouth. His tongue outlined her rounded
nipple, stroked it, teased it. One hand pushed open the front
fold of her wraparound skirt and his fingers boldly glided up
her slender thigh, massaging a path along its inner, most sensitive parts. Her legs began to tremble. His fingers reached the
edge of her bikini panties and toyed with the lacy elastic.

"Yes," she breathed.

As she lifted her hips to help him, he slid her panties down
along her legs, over her tiny feet. He untied the wraparound
skirt at her waist, then drew the folds apart to view her in her
naked splendor.

"My God, Desiree. You're so lovely. So perfect." His voice
was sandpaper-rough. He stretched up over her and fastened his
mouth to hers in a fiery kiss. The pressure and texture of his
hard wiry-haired chest against the sensitive tips of her breasts
sent ripples of exquisite sensation throughout her body. His
hand stroked up the inside of her thigh, ever closer to the center of her femininity.

"Oh, Kyle," she whispered. "Kyle—"

The phone rang.

She felt their bodies stiffen at the same moment. He lifted his
head.

"Don't answer it!" he whispered forcefully.

She lay frozen beneath him. The ring persisted. She glanced
at the bedside clock. It was almost midnight. "Who could it be
at this hour?"

"Does it matter?" He rested his cheek on her breast and
softly trailed his fingertips along her collarbone.

She took a deep breath, trying desperately to think despite
the fire raging throughout her system. "No one would call so
late unless it was important." She turned sideways and reached
for the phone. With a groan he rolled off her.

"Hello?" Her voice was as unsteady as her hand.

"Desiree? Thank God you're home." She recognized the
gravelly voice of Sam, her program director at the station. "The

Board Op just called and got me out of bed. Seems John's stuck on the freeway. There's a tow truck on the way, but he doesn't know what time he'll get there. Dave can only stay another half hour. I need you to substitute until John makes it in."

"This . . . isn't a good time. I can't, really. Did you try Mark or Wayne? Maybe—"

"Wayne's too drunk to stand up straight and I wasn't able to reach Mark or anyone else. Dammit, Desiree, don't give me any excuses. You're the only one I can depend upon."

She let out a deep sigh of frustration. "Okay, Sam. I'll be there as soon as I can." She hung up the phone and jumped up from the bed, trembling.

"What is it?"

"The night-shift deejay has car trouble." She explained what happened as she quickly donned a T-shirt and faded jeans.

He cursed loudly and sat up on the edge of the bed.

"I'm sorry," she said. "I have no choice."

"I know." But his tone said, That doesn't make it any easier to take. He bent down and retrieved his shirt from where it lay on the floor. "Can I drive you to the station and wait for you?"

"No." She struggled to steady both her breathing and her nerves as she fished in her closet for a pair of leather thongs. "It's not practical. I don't know how long I'll be. It might be several hours."

"Then I'll wait for you here." He put on his shirt and began to fasten the buttons.

"*No.*" She swallowed hard, avoiding his gaze as she slipped into the open shoes. If not for the phone call, they would have made love. She felt certain that it would have been wonderful and glorious, but how could she have lived with the pain and loneliness the next day? The next week? The next month? Even if Kyle stayed the weekend, he'd have to return to Seattle on Monday. She didn't want to think about what happened during those months of forced separation from Steve. Sporadic weekend affairs could only end in heartbreak. She'd been hurt before, and she wouldn't be hurt again.

"I think it'd be best if you went back to the hotel," she said.

"What?" The cry was sharp, incredulous. "Are you serious?"

"Yes."

"You're going to kick me out now, after this—" he gestured toward the bed beneath him "—at this hour?"

"You have a hotel room in L.A., don't you?"

"No. I checked out this morning."

Her mouth opened in surprise. "Why? You bought the tickets for tonight's show...you didn't plan to go home today." She said this as statement of fact, not a question.

"Right." He stood up and tucked his shirt into his pants. "I planned to stay here tonight. Maybe the weekend."

She stared at him for a long moment. "You planned to stay here?"

He blew out an exasperated breath. "Not here. In town, in Anaheim. I was going to find a motel closer to your house."

She'd known what he meant. In all fairness, she had to admit she'd led Kyle on. She'd invited him in, responded to his caresses, urged him on when he offered to stop. But she'd been wrong. Now, if she explained everything about her past, if she told him why she was afraid, would he understand? Would he leave? No. He was far too confident, far too stubborn. Her only recourse was to make him angry.

She strove for a carefully controlled tone. "And when exactly did you plan to do that? After you found out whether or not you'd score? I guess that's what the roses and fancy dinner and show were all about. Tempting bait for your well-planned seduction?" She heard him take a sharp breath. She couldn't look at him. "Do you play this little game on all your business trips? Pick up the first woman you find and see how long it'll take her to go to bed with you?"

In her peripheral vision she could see a muscle twitch in his jaw. "Desiree," he said quietly, "I don't make a game of seducing women, on business trips or anywhere else. I took you out the past few nights because I wanted to be with you. It's that simple. I planned to book another room this afternoon, but I never got a chance."

He ran a hand over the back of his neck in a gesture of frustration. "If you need more time...if you're not ready to make love with me yet, that's fine. I understand. I'll sleep on the couch. I won't touch you again. But there's no need to send me packing."

Sleep on the couch? How long could that arrangement last, given the strength of their attraction? How much willpower did she have left? "I don't think you do understand," she said. "I *don't* need more time. I *don't* want to...to sleep with you. Now. *Ever*." She pointed emphatically toward the door, still avoiding his eyes. "I want you to leave. What happened just now was . . . a mistake."

He leaped forward, grabbed her outstretched arm and pulled her against him. "Mistake? It was no mistake, Desiree, and you know it!" His eyes grew cold as he stared down at her. His lips thinned in irritation.

"What kind of game are *you* trying to play? You've been running hot and cold from the moment we met. The last two nights you backed off like a scared rabbit. This afternoon you were only too willing to let me hold you, kiss you. A few minutes ago you responded to me like a woman on fire. You fanned every spark. And now you're telling me to get lost! What kind of woman are you?"

She opened her mouth to protest, but his angry fingers dug into her other arm and imprisoned her against his chest.

"No, don't tell me. I think I already know. When I first heard you on the air, I thought you had a cute act with your sultry voice and all those none-too-subtle sexual innuendos. A clever tease, a saleable radio personality. Until a few minutes ago I thought the *real* you was different. A warm, caring person. Capable of honest emotions. But I see now it's all part of the act."

She gasped, her cheeks stinging as if she'd been slapped. She'd intended to make him angry, but hadn't counted on dealing with such an explosive temper or its wounding effects.

"I've got to hand it to you, Desiree. You're a real pro. No wonder you haven't been to bed with anyone since this mysterious marriage of yours. You've got the technique down to a science. You know how to lead a man on, get him breathless and then cut off his air supply."

He flung himself away from her, as if she was a hot brand searing his flesh. She rocked backward and clutched at her dresser to keep from falling. He grabbed his vest, then stopped in the doorway and fixed her with an icy stare. "Have a *great* weekend, Desiree."

His footsteps pounded against the hall floor. Her stomach lurched as she heard the door slam with ominous finality. Then she buried her face in her hands and began to sob.

"Good riddance!" Desiree slammed down her ceramic mug on the Formica kitchen table. Hot coffee sloshed over the rim, burning her fingers.

"Ouch! Damn, damn, damn!" She grabbed a sponge and cleaned up the spill, then slumped back in her chair, staring moodily at the arrangement of long-stemmed roses next to the open kitchen window. Sunlight sparkled like diamonds on the tall cut-glass vase and burnished the perfect red buds to a velvety sheen. Why did I bother to bring them home from the station, she wondered. I should have just let them stay there and rot!

She hoped Kyle had driven straight to the airport and taken the first flight to Seattle. I don't need him to complicate my life, she told herself. Not now, not ever.

Then why did it take you fifteen minutes to pull yourself together after he left last night? she asked herself. If only she'd let him stay.

No! She clenched her jaw firmly. She ought to be thankful things didn't go any further. The memory of last night's cold shower made her shiver and she wrapped her arms around her chest. When was she last able to think straight? When did she last have a decent night's sleep? When did she last have a thought that didn't revolve around Kyle? If things were this bad after three evenings in his presence and a few breathtaking caresses, what would it be like after they made love?

The now familiar sound of the Maserati engine pulling into the driveway made her jump, startled. He was here? Why? Her stomach knotted with fury. Didn't he get in his final say last night? Then she remembered the jacket and tie still draped over the chair in her living room. Of course! The efficient business-man was coming back to wrap up all the loose ends.

But it was only nine-thirty in the morning! He had his nerve. What if she'd been asleep?

She ran a hand through her hair—at least she'd brushed it—and looked down in dismay at her oldest pair of cutoffs and clinging red T-shirt. She always wore the same thing. He must be sick of seeing her in—

She caught herself. Why should she care what he thought?

Desiree marched across the living room like a drill sergeant about to reprimand his troops. When she heard his knock she flung open the door, ready with a crisp barb about his inconsiderate timing. Her intended remark died on her lips.

In no way did he resemble an angry entrepreneur come to retrieve lost property. In his present casual state of dress he looked like an Olympic athlete, his body trim and firm, his skin lightly kissed by the sun. His consummate masculine beauty produced a shock wave within her of physical pleasure and she stared at him, transfixed, one hand glued to the doorknob.

He wore a navy-blue polo shirt, open at the neck. The short sleeves stretched over his well-formed biceps. His legs, tan and lean beneath crisp white shorts, were braided with flexible-looking muscles and covered with the same curly dark hair that graced his arms and chest. He stood with his legs apart, arms casually at his side. In one hand he carried a small white paper bag. His expression as their eyes collided was apprehensive, hesitant, contrite.

"Hi," he said softly.

"Hi." The raspy high-pitched voice didn't sound like her own.

"I'm glad you're up. I was afraid I'd wake you."

"Oh...no. I...didn't have to work too late. John arrived at about two." She noticed dark circles under his eyes and wondered if she had them too. Her pounding heart told her how glad she was to see him, but she struggled to hold on to her anger. He called you a tease. Incapable of emotion. "Anyway, I always get up early."

"For a Saturday, this is practically the crack of dawn."

"I like getting up at dawn," she lied. "Now that I'm working days, that is. It's a treat to... to watch the sun rise."

"I think I'd agree. But only if I was lying in bed watching the sun rise. With you."

His eyes burned into hers, sending her heart into a skid. Suddenly they were no longer standing like statues in the doorway, talking about the sunrise. They were back in each other's arms last night and he was saying, "You know how I feel about you...I don't want to hurt you, my darling. I only want to love you."

A hot flush washed over her. She'd wanted him last night. She still did. If he said some cruel things in the heat of anger, it was her own fault. She'd made him angry on purpose.

She swallowed hard and glanced down at the paper bag in his hand. "What's in the bag?"

"A peace offering. Freshly baked this morning."

She took the bag he extended. Her heart flinched when he quickly withdrew his hand, as if afraid to touch her. "Oh! Croissants!" she cried with true delight when she looked inside. "I haven't had one of these in ages."

"Okay if I share a couple with you?"

Her cheeks reddened at her lack of courtesy as she stood back and opened the door wide. "Of course."

He stepped inside and pushed the door closed, then took the bag from her hand. "Let me put these in the oven to warm up." He brushed past her to the kitchen, turned on the oven and flipped the croissants onto the cookie sheet inside.

"Would you like a cup of coffee?" she asked.

"You bet. Coffee's one thing I definitely need this morning."

They engaged in small talk at the tiny kitchen table while they sipped their coffee and ate the hot buttery pastries. He made no reference to their argument, and she felt too uncomfortable to bring it up. She wanted to reach out and touch his hand, tell him how sorry she was. But he seemed distant, aloof. Why did he bother to come?

Two cups of coffee later, Kyle sat back in his chair, folded his hands behind his head and heaved a deep sigh. "Okay. We ate. We drank. Now let's be merry."

"Merry?"

"Yes. What we need is to get out and have some fun. And I've got it all arranged. I'm going to take you for a ride in the sky."

A stab of alarm pierced through her. "What do you mean?"

"I arranged to rent a plane from the Long Beach Pilots' Club." He grinned like a child who'd just gotten out of school for the summer. "I'm taking you to Catalina Island for the day."

Seven

Catalina Island?'' Desiree's eyes opened wide in dismay. She'd almost forgotten he had a pilot's license, that he liked to fly. The unpleasant fact had been pushed to the back of her consciousness, and she'd refused to confront it. "You're kidding, aren't you?"

"Why would I be kidding?" Kyle asked.

"Because I . . . I told you, I don't like to fly. Commercial flights are one thing, but I won't go up in a small plane."

"Why not? You'll love it. I promise you." He leaned forward, his elbows on the table, his face eager with excitement. "It's a thrill you can't even imagine until you've tried it."

"Maybe for you. But not for me."

"It could be. You'll never know if you don't give it a chance."

She shook her head. "I won't fly to Catalina Island. I've heard about the airport there. It's dangerous. They have a lot of accidents."

His forehead furrowed in irritation. "Come on. Don't exaggerate. They probably have more accidents on the Santa Ana

Freeway in one week than Catalina Airport sees in a year. Airplane crashes just make the front pages, that's all."

She stood up and trailed her fingers along the smooth cool tabletop. "You may be right. But still—"

"Everything we do involves a risk of some kind," he said sharply. "What's the point in living if you never venture out into new territory, never take any chances? You might as well be dead!"

She took a sharp breath and looked away.

"Look, there's nothing to worry about." He lowered his voice and gestured with an open palm. "I've been flying for thirteen years. I know what I'm doing. And I've made this flight plenty of times before."

"I'm sorry. I don't want to go, Kyle."

He crossed his arms over his wide chest, struggling visibly to keep his patience. "Desiree, I went to a lot of trouble to set this thing up. I've been on the phone since six this morning. I had to pull a few strings to get the plane I wanted on such short notice. I made special arrangements in Catalina…I've got a whole day planned for us. I don't want to cancel it all now."

Irritation prickled up her spine. "I'm sorry you went to so much trouble. Did it ever occur to you I might have other plans today? For all I knew you were back in Seattle by now! If you were going to make all these elaborate arrangements, you should have asked me first!"

"Asked you first? How could I do that, after the way you kicked me out of here last night?" He took a deep breath, but it did little to calm him. "Anyway, this was supposed to be a surprise."

"Well, I'm not going."

"Dammit!" Kyle leaped to his feet. His chair fell to the floor with a crash. "What's with you? Can't you meet a new challenge for once in your life? Don't you have any backbone? You're afraid to get involved with me. You're afraid to go to bed with me. You're afraid to ride in a plane. I'm surprised you have enough nerve to get in your car and drive to work every day!"

"That's not fair!" she shouted. "I have good reasons for not getting involved with you. If it wasn't obvious to you last night, it should be now! And I have just as good a reason for staying out of small airplanes!''

He braced tense fingers on the tabletop. ''What reason?''

''My best friend was killed in a small plane crash! And I almost went with her that day!''

They stared at each other in silence for several moments across the table, his face frozen in shock.

''Her husband was the pilot. They'd only been married a few months. She was . . . only twenty-five.''

A flicker of anguish shone in his eyes. ''I'm sorry,'' he said quietly.

''Pam was like a sister to me.'' Her voice cracked and she cleared her throat before going on. ''When I find myself feeling angry over what happened, when I think what a waste it was she died so young, at the same time I know how relieved I am I didn't go with them. And that makes me feel guilty as hell.''

In two quick strides he moved past the table and took her in his arms. He pulled her against his chest and combed through her silky hair with soothing strokes. ''I'm sorry, Desiree. So sorry. I wish I could take back what I said. I wish I could take away the pain you must feel.''

She released a wavering breath as her arms wrapped around his back. The hot tears that welled up in her eyes were tears of relief, not sorrow. It felt good to be back in his arms again.

''And I'm sorry about last night,'' he said. ''Sorry about everything. I said some ugly things, things I didn't mean. I was frustrated out of my mind. I didn't want to leave, didn't want to spend another minute without you.''

She tilted her head back and met his tortured gaze. ''No, Kyle. Don't apologize. Please. It wasn't your fault, it was mine. I don't know why I flew off the handle like that. I'm sorry.'' She closed her eyes, rested her cheek against his chest and hugged him tightly, yearning for a fiery passionate embrace in return. To her dismay he gave her a single quick squeeze, the kind a brother might give his sister.

''You had every right to react the way you did. I came off like an adolescent maniac. I've been all over you from the moment we met.'' He leaned down and kissed her lightly on the forehead. ''But I promise it'll be different from here on. I won't try to persuade you to do something you're not ready for." He chucked her under the chin. "Okay?"

She smiled weakly as she wiped away a tear, an irrational sense of disappointment flooding her body. "Okay. Sure."

He took a deep breath, then stepped back, met her gaze and held her gently by the shoulders. "Now, will you reconsider? Will you go to Catalina with me today?"

The large white bird stood at attention on the parking strip, wings spread high and wide as if in flight. Turquoise racing stripes were splashed across the body, nose and tail, and sunlight gleamed off the wings. A friendly looking plane, Desiree decided. Maybe this won't be so bad after all.

She leaned against the corrugated aluminum building that housed the Long Beach Pilots' Club and watched Kyle as he checked over the plane, inside and out, in minute detail. There was certainly nothing glamorous about private flying, she decided. Unlike the sleek sophistication and hustle-bustle of a modern commercial airport, the Pilots' Club consisted of one small stark office and a plane-filled parking lot of cracked asphalt, surrounded by a rusting chain-link fence. Still, the idea of hopping into one of these small craft and simply taking off into the air, the way she might take off down the street in her car, filled her as much with excitement as trepidation.

Kyle attached a small metal tow bar to the front of their plane and signaled her to join him. "We need to tow her out of the lot. Grab hold of the wing and pull."

Not wanting to show her surprise, Desiree stepped nimbly up to the front of one wing and grabbed the edge with both hands. The rounded ridge of aluminum felt smooth and cool. As Kyle yanked on the tow bar she lunged backward and gave a mighty tug. To her astonishment the plane rolled forward almost effortlessly.

"Okay, you can let go now," Kyle called. "Just keep an eye on the wing tips. Make sure we're clear of the other planes."

No wonder they call it a light plane, she thought as she watched Kyle tow the plane just past the parking area, her stomach knotting with anxiety. The thing's as flimsy as a child's toy.

"Let's go!" Kyle called a few minutes later.

She ducked down under the wing and opened the cockpit door. "Are you sure this tin can'll make it all the way to Catalina?"

Kyle grinned. "Trust me."

"Do I have any choice?" She smiled stiffly as she climbed up onto the cracked leather seat and slammed the door, thinking, as long as you agreed to do this, show him what a good sport you can be. She settled back in her seat and fastened her safety belt. Myriad gauges and switches, vaguely reminiscent of her console at the studio, covered the black panel before them. The cockpit was tiny, even smaller than the front section of a foreign compact car, she realized with a pang of uneasiness. Well, at least they'd be nice and cozy.

"Do you always do such a thorough check before you take off?" she asked.

"You bet. I'm not taking somebody else's word that this baby's fueled up and in flying condition. I want to see it with my own eyes." He consulted a small handbook on his lap, flipped several switches and leaned out his open window. "Clear!"

A man working on a nearby plane stepped back and waved. Kyle kicked over the starter and the engine sputtered to life. A voice on the radio began to spew out information like a moderator at an auction. She only caught a few intelligible numbers and phrases.

Kyle picked up the hand microphone. "Long Beach Ground, Cessna nine three six five Uniform, Long Beach Pilots. Taxi to two five left with information Echo." After a moment's pause the voice on the radio replied with instructions in the same peculiar language. Kyle hung up the mike and grinned. "Funny. Somehow I feel like you should be talking on this thing."

She laughed, finding his relaxed manner a balm to her growing apprehension. "No way. You talk a different language than any deejay I ever heard. What did they just tell you?"

"The first part was recorded weather information," he said as they taxied toward the runway. "Winds, temperature, altimeter setting. After I identified myself, Ground Control gave me the takeoff point.''

"Sounded like Greek to me."

He laughed. "It's a phonetic alphabet. Helps distinguish one letter from another. Prevents misunderstandings. A is Alpha. B is Bravo. C is Charlie—''

"E is Echo and U is Uniform!'' she finished for him in sudden comprehension.

"Right! Thought you'd be a quick study.'' He flashed her a look of admiration that made her heart sing.

He guided the plane onto the runway and pulled to a halt. As the engine hum increased to a fevered pitch, she stole a glance at Kyle. His mouth curved into a youthful grin and his eyes smoldered with growing excitement. If only he'd look at me that way again, she thought with a twinge of sadness.

He called the tower. Her palms began to sweat and her heart drummed with anticipation. It's going to be okay, she reminded herself. Don't think about what happened to Pam. It was a freak accident. He knows what he's doing.

A radio voice cleared them for takeoff. "Okay, here we go!'' Kyle shouted.

The plane moved forward slowly, then began to pick up speed. The cockpit vibrated. The hum became a roaring buzz in her ears. Desiree grabbed the edge of the seat with rigid arms. Vast open fields raced by on both sides. The tower shot past. The knot in her stomach tightened. Beads of sweat popped out on her brow. Then, suddenly, her stomach dropped as the plane lifted gracefully toward the sky. They were airborne!

"Yee-haw!'' Kyle shouted with childlike glee.

"Wow!'' Desiree heard herself shout. The tension that had built up inside her on the ground released itself in a roar of relieved laughter. The plane was buffeted slightly up and down and the engine continued its loud hum. Mingled with her fear, she felt an unexpected sense of lighthearted giddiness, as if she'd discovered a newfound sense of freedom.

"That wasn't so bad, was it?'' She turned to look out her side window. The plane's high wings allowed an undisturbed view of the ground. Familiar streets and landmarks flashed by, and

Escape with 4 FREE Silhouette Desire Novels (a $9.00 value) and get a Mystery Gift, too!

all at once she felt a sense of smug superiority, floating so freely above all the people and cars stuck on the ground.

"This is great!" she cried, much to her surprise. "We're so low to the ground, it's like a ride at Disneyland!"

He laughed with delight and gave her thigh an affectionate squeeze. "I knew you'd like it."

In what seemed like minutes they were over the ocean. The shimmering, dark-blue water seemed so close she felt she could simply reach out and dip her foot with a sense of peace. She relaxed against her seat with a smile.

"It's beautiful, Kyle." She hoped he'd put his arm around her, draw her close to him. But he didn't. He just looked ahead and smiled, his hands on the controls.

"If you like this, wait until you see Catalina!"

She glanced wistfully at his handsome profile. After the way she'd acted, he was probably afraid she'd turn tail and run again if he got too close. If only he knew how much I yearn for his touch, she thought.

When they reached the island, Kyle circled slowly around it and she held her breath in wonder. No Mediterranean island could be more beautiful than the sight of Santa Catalina as it rose majestically out of the sea. All dark browns and greens against the crystal blue ocean, the island's jagged shoreline was interrupted only by a few small harbors and scattered beaches.

After Kyle received his landing instructions, Desiree eyed the island's mountainous interior with concern. They swept past the island, over the ocean, then circled around the back again.

"Where's the airport?" she asked.

"Right there." He pointed toward a high mountain plateau bisected by a ribbon of asphalt. The short paved road ended at a sharp drop-off and began at the edge of a cliff dropping straight down to the sea.

"That's the runway?" Her mouth went dry. "You're kidding!" But he wasn't. The cliff loomed closer. The engine roar quieted to a low hum. The plane slowed, aimed straight for the cliff's top edge. "Oh, God!" Desiree leaned her head back against the seat and closed her eyes.

"Don't worry! I've done this before, remember?"

She nodded mutely. Nothing to worry about. I am not afraid. She chanted the words over and over to herself. Suddenly she felt a lifting sensation, as if they floated up on a strong breeze. Then the plane drifted downward and touched ground more smoothly than she could have imagined. She could almost feel the brakes grabbing as the plane quickly decelerated, the vibration traveling through her body with blinding force. Just stop before we reach the drop-off at the other side, she prayed silently over the violent pounding of her heart. They slowed to a taxiing speed, then turned and finally rolled to a stop.

She opened her eyes, took a shaky breath and slumped down in the seat.

"Nothing to it, was there?" he grinned.

She smiled weakly. "Piece of cake."

"Fantastic! Everything's here, just the way I wanted it." Kyle tossed the beach bag they'd brought into the trunk of the dark-blue sedan.

"What have you got in there?" Desiree took a step toward the back of the car but he shut the trunk with a clang.

"A surprise. You'll see."

He opened the car door for her and she slid into the bucket seat. At his direction, she'd put on her bathing suit under her shorts and red T-shirt in the airport rest room. He now wore sleek navy-blue bathing trunks, which matched his shirt.

"How did you manage to get this car?" she asked after he'd climbed in and shut the door. "I understood they don't rent cars on the island."

His eyes glittered mysteriously. "They don't."

"You must know someone who lives here, then."

"Several people." He started the engine and headed out of the airport lot.

"Really?" Suddenly she noticed he wasn't taking the road leading to Avalon, the island's only town. "Where are you going?"

"You've been to Avalon before, right?"

"Yes." She had taken a one-day cruise to Catalina two years before. She'd spent the afternoon with hordes of other sightseers combing through the shops and museum in the small harbor town.

"So have I. I can only take so much of that touristy stuff. I have something completely different in mind for us today."

The narrow winding road hugged the dry desolate mountain on one side and dropped off sharply on the other. The terrain resembled a desert wilderness, mostly scrub oak, rock and cacti. The car had no air conditioner and she was beginning to get uncomfortably hot. Then they rounded a bend and she caught sight of a small lonely stretch of sand beach below rocky cliffs. He turned onto a bluff above the beach and parked next to the only other car there.

"Oh, Kyle, how wonderful!" She jumped out of the car, ran to the edge of the bluff and gazed down with growing excitement at the sparkling white sand and gently rolling surf beyond. The sun blazed in the cloudless sky over an endless shimmering blue sea. The only people in sight were packing up their things and heading up the winding path along the cliffs.

"I've never seen a beach so empty on a Saturday! Why isn't anyone else here?" she asked.

Kyle stepped up beside her and draped an arm casually across her shoulder. "Tourists can't rent cars so the only people who can get here are the islanders, and there's not many of those. This is the smallest beach, and the farthest from town, so I figured it wouldn't be too crowded." He raised an inquiring eyebrow in her direction. "Like it?"

Yesterday he'd have wrapped his arms around her waist, held her and whispered that question against her ear. She sighed and turned to look up at him. "It's incredible. Like being—" She laughed. "I know it's silly, but it's like being shipwrecked on a desert island. It's paradise!"

He turned her around to face him. "I hoped you'd feel this way. I was here once on my own, several years ago. I've always dreamed of coming back, when I had someone special to share it with."

She stood on her tiptoes, clasped her hands behind his neck and kissed him. "I'm glad I'm the special someone you chose."

He reached up to clasp both her wrists in his hands. Although he didn't kiss her in return, she could tell her reaction pleased him by the soft glow in his green eyes. "So am I," he whispered. "So am I."

"Now *here's* what I call an ideal picnic spot." Kyle set down the red ice chest and wicker basket next to the rocky cliff and pulled a folded blanket out of the beach bag.

Desiree helped him spread the large soft blanket across the smooth sand, then stood up to admire the spot they'd found. At the far end of the beach, the little sandy alcove dipped in under the shade of dark overhanging rocks, which hid from view the bluff high above. Just a dozen yards away the surf lapped the shore, but here the sand was fine, soft and white.

"I can't wait to try the water," she said. The hot sun, like a giant oven, baked her back and shoulders through her T-shirt.

Kyle peeled off his shirt. She couldn't resist a glance at the rippling muscles of his smooth tanned back as he raised his arms over his head. She wanted to steal up behind him, touch the curved shoulder blades of his broad upper back and curl her arms about his slim waist. Would he hug her back? Or would he only laugh and shrug her off? He turned around to face her and she quickly averted her eyes.

"How about if we eat first? This engine won't run much longer on the skimpy continental breakfast we ate this morning."

Suddenly aware of a ravenous ache in her stomach, she laughed and plopped down on the blanket, Indian-style. "Sounds great. But I hope you've got a horse in there. I think I could eat one."

He knelt down and opened the lid of the picnic basket. "Sorry, no horses today. We've got everything but." He lifted out a small French bread, several knives, a wooden cutting board, plastic plates and utensils. From the cooler he produced three kinds of cheese, a salami, a tin of pâté de fois gras, green grapes, apples, a jar of black olives and a relish tray. Finally he pulled out a frosty bottle of champagne and two stemmed glasses.

"Where did you get all this?" she cried in amazement.

"I told you I was up at six o'clock making phone calls." He handed her a chilled glass, then expertly opened the bottle and filled her glass with the sparkling clear wine. At her puzzled look he added, "The owner of the Avalon Grand Hotel is a friend of mine. He had the restaurant put this together for us. Oh, and one more thing." He reached back in the cooler and lifted up a six-pack of Sparkle Light soda pop. "In case you're still thirsty after the champagne," he grinned.

She laughed in delight. "Lucky me, to know someone with such terrific connections!"

When he'd filled his own glass he raised it to hers in a toast. "To the most beautiful exciting woman I've ever met, and four unforgettable days."

Unforgettable days. Desiree hoped he couldn't see her silent pang of disappointment at his words. If only he'd said, *To many more wonderful days like this.* But then, hadn't she made it clear she thought that impossible?

Desiree clinked her glass lightly against his, smiling facetiously. "To the best pilot I've ever entrusted my life to."

She took a sip of the crisp tangy wine and sighed in satisfaction as she felt the refreshing coolness revitalize her system. They feasted on the assortment of delicacies, enjoyed the cool shade under the overhanging cliff, the sound of the rolling waves and the pleasant fresh scent of the clean sea air. After they packed up the leftovers, Kyle dipped back into the cooler, brought out two small covered bowls and handed one to Desiree with a flourish.

"Ta da! *La pièce de résistance.*"

"Chocolate mousse!" Desiree cried. "How did you know it's my favorite?"

He laughed. "A lucky guess. It's my favorite, too."

Desiree picked up a spoon and dove in. A mesmerized smile crossed her face as she savored the cold creamy chocolate. "Mmm, this is heaven. I've been *dying* for chocolate the past two days."

He sat up, scooted next to her, and slid one hand under her shirt to rest on her waist. "A bona fide chocaholic, huh?"

She nodded. "In the worst possible way."

She felt herself tremble under the touch of his fingers against her bare skin. *Desiree, your skin is so soft,* he'd said last night. *Like silk . . .*

As if afraid he was getting too close, Kyle withdrew his hand and reached for the champagne bottle. "Shall we finish this off?"

All night I've been dying to hold you... kiss you... touch you like.... Would he ever say those words to her again? She swallowed over the lump in her throat. "You bet."

He emptied the bottle into their glasses. They sat side by side on the blanket, finished their desert and sipped the bubbly wine. Desiree glanced at his bare thigh, so close to her own. *There's nothing more beautiful than what we feel for each other right now,* he'd told her. *I don't want to hurt you, my darling. I only want to love you.*

The thought came unbidden, from nowhere yet she realized, with a start, that it had smoldered at the edge of her consciousness for the past few days, waiting for her to acknowledge it. In the short time they'd been together, she'd come to feel closer to Kyle than to anyone she'd ever known. Somehow, without intending to, she was falling deeply, irrevocably in love with him.

"Penny for your thoughts."

Her head whipped up. "What? Oh, I was just thinking how beautiful it is here. And how much I've enjoyed everything."

He drained his glass and set it back in the basket. "Even the flight?"

"Yes. Even the flight." She stared at the blanket beneath them, suddenly unable to look at him. "It was a thrill," she admitted. "The biggest thrill I've ever experienced."

His voice had a teasing lilt to it. "The biggest thrill?"

She couldn't believe she blushed. "Yes. The biggest thrill."

He leaned forward and kissed her lightly on the lips. "I'm glad. Now what do you say we go jump in that water?"

"All right." She shook her head to clear it, then pushed herself to a stand. As she shrugged quickly out of her top and shorts, she heard his soft whistle.

"Nice bathing suit." His eyes slid down her body, took in the rise of her breasts above the skimpy royal-blue-and-white bikini top, the soft curves of her waist and hips, the triangular wisp of fabric below. He cleared his throat and grinned devilishly. "But I won't complain if you take it off. I doubt anyone will come by. The cliff's too rocky and there's no path at this end of the beach. And the only creatures who are likely to happen by from the ocean side are the feathered variety."

"No way!" she cried indignantly. "If you want to skinny dip, you can do it by yourself!"

"You've got yourself a deal." To her surprise and dismay, he took her at her word. In one downward swoop he divested himself of his bathing trunks and tossed them aside.

She only had a brief instant to stare, breathless, at his perfect golden body before he grabbed her hand and pulled her with him into the sparkling waves. She gasped as the cold water splashed against her legs, then enveloped her to the waist. She would have preferred to proceed more slowly, to take a few minutes to adjust to the water. But Kyle mercilessly plunged ahead, refusing to let go of her hand.

She couldn't prevent her eyes from darting toward the naked virile form beside her. Were the sudden shivers traveling up her spine due to the brisk water temperature, or to the sight of Kyle's splendid masculinity so casually displayed?

Finally he let go of her hand and dove forward under a wave. He emerged a few feet beyond, spraying water and laughing. "Want to swim out a ways?"

"Sure!" A strong swimmer, Desiree knifed forward through the water. Her body gradually adjusted to the water, which now felt delightfully invigorating. They swam out side by side for a time, rising up to crest each gentle wave, then turned and rode the tide back in. When he reached a spot where he could touch bottom, he stopped and pulled her into his arms.

"Fantastic, isn't it?"

In answer she wrapped her arms around his neck, laughing and nodding. Suddenly their eyes met and she felt him stiffen, as if struggling to keep his emotions in check. Desiree's heart beat a jagged rhythm as they bobbed up and down together on the waves. His eyes seemed to echo his words of last night. *You know how I feel about you. I've made no secret of it. Do you feel the same way about me?* Yes! her mind cried. Yes! Can't you see? I love you! I adore you!

He brought one hand up to the nape of her neck and kissed her lightly. With a small moan she parted his lips with her tongue and deepened the kiss, sighing with pleasure as he wrapped his tongue around hers. A lightning bolt of desire flashed through her body, touching each vital organ, the tips of her breasts, the center of her womanhood. His arms tightened around her as he kissed her fiercely, ravenously. He brought up one hand to cover her full aching breast, kneaded it gently, working his way to the crest, which strained toward his caressing fingers. The ocean lapped and rolled against them, a frenzied counterpoint to their mounting passion.

"You're lovely, Desiree. Every perfect inch of you."

He fused her mouth to his once more and she lifted her legs to clasp tightly around his waist. *You are Desiree... Desired. Wanted. Longed for.* A shiver passed through her body as she felt his naked manhood, hard with desire, press against the very cove of her femininity. She might as well have been naked, too, for all the protection her thin bikini bottoms provided between them. *Let me show you how much I care. Let me make love to you.* With sudden force he freed her mouth, and she felt rather than heard his passionate groan.

"Desiree," he whispered thickly into her ear. "Can you feel how much I want you?"

And I want you. The acknowledgement came from deep in her soul and she wrapped her arms more tightly around him, as if by holding him close he could never leave her side. What's the point in living if you never take risks, he'd said this morning. They lived separate lives, could only share a brief instant in time together. But somehow it didn't matter anymore. She knew what was to come would be sweet and precious, a treasure to look back on all the years of her life. They were meant for each other now; this moment was as inevitable as the ebb and flow of the swirling tide.

Her voice was a soft plea against his ear. "Make love to me."

Eight

She was grateful he didn't hesitate or give her a chance to question her decision. He carried her out of the water and across the sand, laid her down on the soft wide blanket in the shelter of the cliff. He stretched out beside her and held her for a long moment before he kissed her, his hands combing through the wet hair streaming across her shoulders.

She relished the feel of his cool wet body against hers, drank in his clean scent and savored the salty taste of his skin beneath her lips. She felt her heart drumming riotously beneath her breast and knew he must feel it, too. When he bent his head to kiss her, his lips moved softly, earnestly, slowly over hers. Each light touch of his mouth was like a mind-stealing drug, warming and soothing her already willing body and brain.

As she returned his kiss, her hands massaged the smooth firm muscles of his slippery wet back, which flexed with each movement of his arms and body against hers. He ran his fingers the length of her slender back to the edge of her bikini bottoms, then up again, to the ties holding her top. With a single tug he untied the bow at her back. He kissed her once more, leisurely, as if to savor each tiny moment and heighten their pleasure by prolonging the anticipation. At last he drew back and lifted the wisp of fabric over her head. He gently rolled her to her back, swept his fingers over her bare breasts and down the curves of her waist, then nimbly removed her bikini bottoms.

She lay submissive beneath him, marveling over her lack of embarrassment. Never in her life had she felt such pride in her body. A thrill raced through her under Kyle's impassioned gaze.

"You're a goddess," he whispered, eyes shining with tenderness and delight. With loving fingers he traced the inside of both her thighs, and she caught her breath as he ruffled the tangle of curls above.

She looked at his sleek masculine body, the powerful chest, the corded muscular legs, the dusting of wiry hair over lightly tanned skin. "You're beautiful," she said. "All day I've wanted to touch you, hold you."

A smile twitched his lips as he lay suddenly still beside her, propped on one elbow. "Please. Feel free."

Hesitantly she sifted through the satiny line of hair that trailed down the center of his chest and circled the dimple of his navel with an inquisitive finger. She felt his stomach contract, heard his rapid intake of breath. Emboldened by his response, she moved her hand lower, and lower still. And then—

A distant sharp cry suddenly broke the stillness. She yanked back her hand and froze in confusion.

"Desiree . . . ? What is it?"

The sharp cry rang again, all at once familiar and not at all frightening. She turned her head, saw the sea gull swoop low over the cliffs, flap his wings and drop to the sand a few yards away. Then, just as suddenly as he had come, the bird spread his wings and darted away across the waves.

She looked back at Kyle, touching his cheek with her hand. "The sea gull. It . . . startled me." To her surprise she felt herself blush, shiver. Why? She wasn't shy or cold.

He grasped her hand in his, turned it against his lips and kissed each one of her knuckles in turn. "Are you afraid?" he asked softly.

She bit her bottom lip to stop it from quivering. Was she afraid? It had been so very long. His entire body spoke of his longing for her, and the fire which burned within her loins told her how much she wanted him. But would she be able to please him? Her intimacies with Steve had been sweet and satisfying but hardly daring or innovative, and she had very little other experience. Would Kyle be disappointed in her?

As if sensing her distress, he smoothed her wet hair back from her forehead, his eyes smiling a silent endearment. "What is it? Does it feel strange to lie here with me, on the beach?"

No, she thought. It feels right. Oh, so right. The overhanging rocks sheltered them from view above, and the distant rolling surf played a melodious symphony beneath the canopy of the bright blue sky. It was as if this secluded shaded alcove was meant for them alone.

"Do you want to stop? To wait until we get home?" His low voice was concerned.

She felt tears start in the corner of her eyes as a rush of affection welled in her throat. Twice now she'd told him to stop, forced him to leave when his desire for her was all too evident. Still he was willing to call it off now if she was uncertain. She'd never met anyone so understanding, so unselfish. His eyes as they met hers were filled with a yearning that surpassed sexual desire. He wanted her. But not just her body. He cared about her, her needs, her feelings. Her heart went out to him wholly.

"I don't want to stop," she whispered. "I'm just a little nervous."

"Don't be. Relax. Just enjoy the pleasure we can give each other."

Their mouths touched tentatively at first, as his fingers cupped her breast and paid loving attention to its rose-colored peak. Her hands moved caressingly up and down his sides, acquainting themselves with the lean hardness of his hips and hair-roughened thighs. Then their lips began to move faster, faster. Tongues delved, tasted, explored, driven by hunger and the need to fulfill their long-restrained passion.

Her hands roved down his back, cupped his firm buttocks and pulled him more tightly against her. She felt his urgent desire, like a shaft of velvet-covered steel, press hard against her thigh. He groaned low and deep in his chest as he kissed the corners of her lips, her cheeks, the length of her throat.

"Oh, Kyle. Kyle."

Their breath came in quick gasps now as their hands moved over each other without restraint, each caress becoming bolder, more intimate. His nibbling teeth against her sensitive neck brought every cell in her body to full jolting awareness. His mouth moved with seductive slowness across her shoulders, over the outer curve of her breast, then closed around the nipple aching with desire. She wound her fingers through his damp hair, held his head against her breast as he sucked sweetly, his tongue revolving tantalizingly around the taut bud.

His palm prowled across her ribcage and abdomen, then lower, ever closer to the ultimate goal. And then he was there. Questing fingers gently parted her thighs, sought, found. Tremors shot through her as his fingers probed the pulsing source of her passion, mesmerizing her with their gentle accuracy. She writhed beneath him in ecstasy, a hot molten core of need, mindless to everything but the tributes his hands and lips paid her body. I want you, I want you, her body sang. Now! Now!

With an impassioned groan, she curled her fingers around his hard biceps, pulling him up on top of her. There was no need to speak. Their eyes locked, communicating their mutual hunger more eloquently than words. With trembling fingers she reached down, encircled him, guiding him into the inviting silk of her body. She felt a sensation of piercing tightness, an injection of smooth liquid fire that blended with the flames raging within her, and she whimpered with joy and relief.

"Desiree...darling..." he whispered against her lips, his eyes filled as much with passion as compassion. "Does it hurt? Tell me."

"No." It did, but it was a welcome pain, and she knew it wouldn't last long. She moved against him, pulling him more deeply into the tight moistness. His body molded perfectly to hers, like two missing pieces of a puzzle finally joined.

"You feel wonderful," he whispered. "So soft. Warm."

The hurt gave way to a sweet violent throbbing as she matched his body's rhythmic movements with her own, bring-

ing him closer and closer to her center. She heard the call of a
gull again, and the lulling sound of the waves seemed to sur-
round her. She opened her eyes for an instant to the brilliant
blue sky, then shut them again, nearly bursting with the joy of
having him within her in this beautiful magical place. Each
thrust of his body sent her further and further into a realm of
uncharted ecstasy. Did it ever feel like this before? she wondered. Ever?

He moved harder, faster, until she felt her body tense with
anticipation, vibrate with impending need. For an instant she
froze, suspended in time, and then in a burst of light she broke
free, her body pulsing with climactic shudders, which carried
her high into the air.

She cried out, and at the same time, from far away, she heard
his soft moans. Then she felt his entire body tauten as he
gripped her tightly, calling her name. She wrapped herself
around him, her mind floating freely, her body reveling in his
closeness and warmth. Then ever so slowly, they drifted together back to earth.

Many minutes passed as they held each other, panting to regain their breath. She opened her eyes and smiled into his. The
corner of his mouth lifted up in a grin. He rolled them gently
to their sides, bodies still clinging together, arms and legs entwined, tips of noses touching. She caressed his cheek lovingly
with her palm, tried to memorize the texture of his skin, the
exact slope of his nose, the angles of his cheek and jaw.

"I take it back, Kyle," she said at last, a teasing gleam in her
amber eyes.

"What?"

"The plane ride today was only the second most thrilling
experience of my life."

She felt her grin start just as his shoulders began to shake.
Then, together, eyes shining, heads thrown back, they laughed
out loud.

Desiree awoke and stretched lazily. A sleepy smile curved her
lips and she was filled with a sense of contentment, although
she couldn't at first remember why. Then, as memories of the
night flooded her mind, her eyes snapped open. She saw the

empty pillow beside her and an ache swept over her. Where was he?

A low cheerful whistle and the sound of running water drifted in from the kitchen. Making coffee, she surmised with a sigh of relief. She relaxed beneath the covers and closed her eyes.

It was a night she'd never forget. Just thinking about it made her feel faint with pleasure. They had returned from the island just before dark, still glowing from their passionate encounter on the beach and had taken a long luxurious shower together.

"I could make love to you all night long, and it still wouldn't be enough," Kyle said as he rubbed a soft thick towel over every inch of her body.

She smiled alluringly. "Try me."

And so he did. They made love again and again, and each time was better than the last, each climax more earth-shaking than the one before. He carried her to heights of ecstasy she'd never dared to dream of, all the while treating her with caring and tenderness, aware of her every need and desire.

Sometimes, after they looked into each other's eyes and laughed, as they had that afternoon, overwhelmed by the sense of pure joy that enveloped them. Other times they slept, wrapped in the warm cocoon of each other's arms, only to awaken in the moonlit darkness more filled with desire than before.

"You're so beautiful, so giving," he'd said as he cradled her against his chest. "How was I lucky enough to find you?"

"I've never known anyone like you, Kyle. It's never been like this for me before."

"For me either. My lovely Desiree..."

Never in her life had she felt so beautiful, so idolized. He awakened desires within her she'd never believed existed, made her feel voluptuous, feminine, from the tips of her toes to the very roots of her hair.

"Touch me," he said. "There. Ahh, that's it. Perfect. If you only knew how good that feels...."

Her marriage bed had been chaste and adolescent compared to the loving she shared with Kyle. It seemed there was no part of her body left untouched by the warm pressure of his lips, the magic of his fingers.

"Your skin is so soft. Smooth. Feminine. I love the way it feels here. And here."

"And you're so hard. Everywhere. Especially here."

He chuckled softly. "Do you like...this?"

"Like it? Oh, Kyle..."

As she thought back over everything she'd said, every wanton thing she'd done, her cheeks flushed hotly. Was the woman who behaved with such unashamed abandon last night really her? Desiree? Yes, and she'd loved every second of it!

She threw off the sheet, stretched her arms and legs and grinned happily to herself. She couldn't remember when she'd ever so looked forward to a new day. She'd slept very little; she ought to feel exhausted. But instead she felt completely revitalized.

She heard soft footsteps in the hall and propped herself up with her arms. Her amber eyes glimmered in the morning sunlight, which filtered through the eyelet curtains. He stepped in quietly, wearing only his navy-blue bathing trunks and carrying a dark brown leather garment bag. He stopped when he saw her, as if momentarily stunned. She had no idea how appealing she looked, her shapely legs stretched out before her, tousled hair provocatively framing her face, cheeks still flushed with a sleepy-warm glow, her milky-white breasts soft and alluring.

"Good morning," he said, his voice so low and rough she barely caught the words.

"Good morning." She greedily feasted her eyes on each well-sculpted muscle, each detail of the strong masculine body she'd come to know so well.

"I hope you don't mind if I...hang up a few things. This has been sitting out in the car for two days."

"Please, be my guest." She swung her legs off the bed and sidled over to him.

He opened her closet, hung his garment bag inside. Unzipping the case, he moved two suits and shirts out onto the closet rod. They looked hopelessly wrinkled.

Her arms encircled his waist. "You can't wear those. We'll have to iron them."

He shook his head. "Don't worry about it. They'll spring back to life by tomorrow."

"You think so?"

He drew her against his chest. "I do."

"But what will you wear today?"

"Nothing."

"Nothing?"

"Absolutely nothing." He kissed her languorously. Heaving a deep sigh of pleasure, he said, "By the way, I was right."

"About what?" she half-whispered, half-moaned.

"We made love all night long, and it still wasn't enough." With an animallike growl he picked her up, threw her onto the bed and leaped on top of her.

"Help!" she cried. "Wait, Kyle, wait! We haven't eaten since lunch yesterday at the beach. I'm starving. I've got to eat something."

He leered wickedly into her eyes. "I can think of something I'd like to nibble on right now. But I'll settle for this." He pretended to take a bite out of her shoulder. She writhed with laughter beneath him, finally managing to roll away from him and drop off the side of the bed. Taking a few steps backward, she grabbed her hairbrush from the dresser and brandished it like a weapon. "Come near me again and I'll strike where you'll most regret it," she cried, her eyes flashing dangerously.

"Please. Not that!" He stopped, stood up and raised his palms. "I surrender! Truce! We'll take a break. We'll eat. But first, I have to run."

"Run?"

He nodded. "Run. As in jog. You know, that's where you move your feet quickly across the floor like this." He darted around the bed and, lunging forward, grabbed her. Her scream ended abruptly as his mouth came down on hers. He kissed her soundly, then released her mouth, his breath warming her lips. "Don't you ever run?"

"Not very often," she said breathlessly.

"I jog every morning the sun shines," he said, still holding her in his arms. "And that's not often enough for me in Seattle. I want to make the most of your gorgeous weather while I'm here. Want to join me?"

His reference to his hometown sent a stab of pain piercing through her chest, reminding her of how short their time together would be. Her smile faded. "I'd...love to run with you. Let me just put on some...some clothes."

They did warm-up exercises together on her living-room floor, then jogged through her neighborhood to a nearby park. She kept pace with him easily and found herself enjoying the warm sunshine, the smell of the freshly mown grass. She tried not to look at Kyle as they ran, tried to push the thought of his leaving out of her mind.

More than once, during their lovemaking the night before, she'd wanted to burst out with a heartfelt I love you, Kyle. His own whispered endearments had made her feel she was as special to him as he'd become to her. But never once did he say he loved her. How could she admit to him the depths of her feelings, when she wasn't certain if he returned them?

Let's just take things one day at a time, he'd said the other night. Maybe a few days together was all he had in mind. After he left on Monday, would she ever see him again? Of course you will, she told herself. Don't be ridiculous. But when? How often? And for how long?

She wondered if he often spent weekends away from home this way. How many women had enjoyed the delights of his lovemaking, the passionate warmth of his embrace? Don't think about it, she cautioned herself. It suddenly became a Herculean task to draw breath into her lungs as she ran. Just enjoy the little time you have.

After they returned and took an invigorating shower, they made a breakfast feast together in her cozy kitchen. Kyle, his tanned back magnificent above a pair of white tennis shorts, stood at the stove and cooked a delicious fluffy omelet filled with tomatoes and cheese. After throwing on a pale blue tube top and lavender-blue-and-black Hawaiian-print shorts, she prepared freshly squeezed orange juice, hot coffee, toasted buttered English muffins and crisply fried ham. They ate at her

tiny kitchen table, crowded by the huge vase of red roses he'd
sent three days before.

"Nice flowers," Kyle said as he speared a piece of ham with
his fork. "Where'd you get those? Some love-sick fan?"

"Sick is not the word. The man's a maniac." She grinned at
him across the table. "He hasn't let me sleep for the past four
nights."

"Four nights?" His eyes narrowed with mock jealousy. "I
can vouch for the fact you didn't get any sleep last night. But
what about the three nights before?"

She laughed as she reached under the table to caress his bare
thigh. "Who could sleep, after the way you kissed me after our
walk on the beach? And then Friday, after our...argu-
ment—"

He seized her hand, squeezed it. "Let's not talk about that.
It's past. Forgotten." He thumped the chipped edge of the
Formica table with his fork. "Why do you have this awful table, anyway? Everything else in this house is a beautiful antique."

"You mean you don't like my fifties-style pink Formica?
What's wrong with you?"

"Pink? What do you mean, pink? The table's white."

"It's pink."

He bent closer, staring at the tabletop. "Really? Pink?"

"Pink. Pale pink."

"It looks white to me." He shrugged, then shook his head.
"Good grief, a pink Formica table. And I thought white was
bad."

She frowned with feigned indignation. "This table's the
height of chic. The epitome of class. Besides, it—"

"Was my great-grandmother's," they finished in unison. He
rolled his eyes. She nodded sheepishly.

"I realize you were named after her...which I'm grateful for,
by the way," he said, pointing his fork at her. "It's a beautiful
name. But you didn't have to take every piece of furniture she
had, for God's sake! This is an atrocity. Look at this crack
along the edge. Why don't you get a nice table? Mahogany, to
match your living-room set? Your dining room is practically
empty."

"I suppose I should. I just never had any reason to. I don't have people over for dinner very often." She finished the last of her muffin and coffee. "I haven't bought any furniture in years. I've had to move too often. This is sturdy, and I don't have to worry if it gets slightly banged up."

"Doesn't it bother you? Having to move all the time?"

She shrugged. "Comes with the territory. Radio's a part of me I can't give up. Moving's a condition I've had to accept."

"What about now? You said you don't ever plan to leave Orange County. Does that mean you think KICK will keep you on indefinitely?"

She laughed. "Fat chance. There's no such word as *indefinitely* in a radio station's vocabulary." She toyed with her empty coffee cup, finally lifting her eyes to his. "But I'm here, now. I have a terrific job, and good jobs are hard to come by. I'll stay as long as they'll keep me."

His eyes burned into hers across the table. He opened his mouth to speak, then seemed to think better of it. He took a deep breath, leaned his elbows on the table and enfolded her slender hands between his large firm ones.

"So tell me, what is it that's so exciting about being a deejay? I should think you'd get tired of working in that tiny studio, day after day, playing the same songs over and over."

"True. I love most everything about the business, but there is a burnout factor. After you've talked about a song twenty-five times, it's pretty hard to think up something original to say. Even so, it's—"

He stretched out her arm, leaned across the small table and dropped damp sucking kisses along its length in a path toward her shoulder. "It's what?"

She swallowed hard, finding it increasingly difficult to think, as exquisite chills shivered up and down her arms. "It's...exciting, stimulating...." His lips reached her shoulder and he stood up, cradled her neck with his hand and pulled her closer across the table. When his tongue flicked over the sensitive spot at the side of her throat, she drew a wavering breath.

"And because I can be beautiful on the air. Special. I can stir people's imagination."

"You don't need to go on the air for that," he whispered. "You're very special in person. Beautiful. Exciting." He slipped his index finger over the edge of her tube top at her cleavage and tugged downward. The top dropped and her pert breasts flexed out to his admiring view. "Stimulating," he rasped. He stepped around the table and pulled her into his arms. With a gasp she felt the solid ridge of his masculinity burrow into her abdomen.

"And you definitely stir my imagination," he said as he covered her mouth with his.

"What do you do about clothes?"

"Clothes?"

"Yes." Desiree tipped the last of the ice-cold Chablis into the etched stemmed glass in Kyle's hand. "If you can't see certain colors, how do you know what clothes go together?"

Darkness had just descended. They'd spent the afternoon in and out of bed. Mostly in. They'd ignored the outside world, as if nothing existed but the two of them and the feelings they shared in this tiny stolen moment in time. Since it had been too hot to cook, Desiree had made an enormous chef's salad for dinner, which she'd served with the bottle of Chablis she'd put in the refrigerator that morning.

Now, their appetite sated, they relaxed together in the redwood swing on her back patio. The cool night air, perfumed with the scent of orange blossoms from the tree in her backyard, felt delightfully refreshing. They'd each donned a pair of shorts and T-shirt, and Desiree wore the golden songbird pendant Kyle admired on their first date.

"I don't. I have to rely on what the salesclerks tell me at the store, buy things as a set and always wear them that way. I stick to gray, blue and brown whenever possible."

She was silent for a moment, savoring the wine's delicate aroma and dry tangy taste. "It must be frustrating."

"At times." He grinned. "When I was a kid, my sisters used to play jokes on me, mix up the clothes in my drawer so I wore things that looked ridiculous together. I still have a lot of trouble with socks. Telling the dark browns from the blacks and greens."

She giggled. "You need a wife to help you dress." The moment she said the words she regretted them. His eyes opened wide. His eyebrows lifted. He studied her with earnest amusement.

"Maybe I do."

What a stupid thing to say! She averted her eyes, cleared her throat. "Your sisters . . . it wasn't very nice, what they did."

He shrugged. "I made up for it. One night when I was a senior in high school, the oldest four girls were sitting around the living room in bathrobes and curlers, with mud masks plastered all over their faces. They were in their teens at the time. I called up a bunch of my friends and asked them to come over, guys they all had crushes on."

"Oh, Kyle! You didn't!"

"I did."

Desiree threw her head back and burst out with laughter. "They must have died of embarrassment. They must have killed you!"

He nodded, grinning. "I was blacklisted for months."

"You're a real devil, you know that?"

He sipped his wine, watching his fingertip trail along her shoulder and down her arm. A quiet sadness filled his eyes and his voice as he said, "I'm going to miss you."

His sudden change of mood caught her off-guard and brought a lump to her throat. She looked away. Why was he bringing it up now? She knew this was their last evening together, but she'd avoided thinking about it, the way one avoids thinking about the inevitable end of a wonderful vacation. You know it'll be over soon, and you'll have to go home. But you put it out of your mind. You don't let it spoil your fun.

"I'll . . . miss you, too," she said softly.

"I wish things were different. I wish I didn't live so far away, that we could—"

"It's okay." Suddenly the wine tasted bitter. She set down her glass next to the swing. "You don't have to explain."

"I do. I want you to know how much this weekend's meant to me. You're a beautiful special woman, Desiree. I care for you a great deal. It's not going to be easy going back, putting myself through the usual routine, knowing you're over a thousand miles away."

She pressed her lips together, not trusting herself to speak.

He drained his glass and set it down. Gently taking her into his arms, he caressed her shoulders and ran his lips over her silky hair. "I wish I could stay longer, but I can't. I've got an important meeting tomorrow afternoon. I have to leave first thing in the morning."

"I understand. I didn't expect you to stay longer." Her voice cracked and she inhaled a sobbing breath as tears welled up in her eyes.

"Don't cry, sweetheart. Don't cry."

"I'm not." She squeezed her eyes shut, swallowed hard and willed the threatening tears to dissolve. "I...knew we only had a few days together, that you'd have to go back. I tried so hard, at first, not to get involved with you because I knew it couldn't last. But I—"

"What?" He pulled back and stared at her. "Who said it couldn't last?"

"You know it can't. You said, at the beginning, let's take things one day at a time. So I did. But where can it go from here? What kind of future could we build, with you in Seattle and me here?"

"We'll make it work," he said emphatically.

She shook her head. "How? How often could we see each other?"

"Weekends. Every single weekend. Plenty of couples who live in the same town don't see each other more often than that."

"Every weekend? How can we? It'd cost a fortune!"

"Who cares? I'll pay for the airline tickets, the phone bills. I'll even do all the traveling if you want."

"You can't do that. You can't fly down here every single weekend!"

"I can and I will."

She shook her head. "We'll only make each other miserable."

"I expect to be miserable five days every week. But we're going to live gloriously on the weekends." He slid next to her, stretched one arm behind her along the back of the swing. He lifted the songbird pendant at her throat, held it up to the moonlight and studied it. "And I may have another excuse to come down here. Often."

"Why?"

"I flew down originally for a meeting with a potential client. But while I was here, I took a look at a manufacturing plant in L.A. I'm considering buying it."

"Really?"

"Yes. I expect to make a decision in the next week or two." He took one of her hands in his and squeezed it. "If I do buy the company, I'll be flying down for a week at a time, especially at first while things are getting set up."

A small flame of hope lit up inside her. Could it be true? A week at a time? Then the flame died down and a voice inside her cried, What difference would it make? Someday you'd have to leave. Who knows where you'll end up? And you'll be back where you started.

He cupped her cheek in his hand and caressed her with his gaze. "But no matter what happens, I'll be down here as often as I can to see you. Believe that."

A lone tear trickled down her cheek. "I do. I believe you mean it now." She grasped his hand, pulled it away from her face and held it in her lap. "But it won't last, Kyle. One of us will be hurt in the end."

He sighed in exasperation. "Dammit, you've been fighting me at every turn from the moment we met! Why? Didn't this weekend mean anything to you? Can't you even give an inch? Don't you care enough about me to even try to make this work?"

"Yes! I care about you!" she cried. "More than any man I've ever met! And I'll be miserable the moment you leave! But a long-distance relationship can't work. It's impossible!"

"How do you know it's impossible?" he asked fiercely. "Have you ever tried it?"

"Yes!"

"When?"

"When I left my husband!"

Nine

A tense silence reigned for several moments. Desiree stared straight ahead at the dark stretch of yard beyond the patio light's glow, unwilling to meet his gaze.

"Tell me, Desiree," he said finally, his voice soft and deep. "Tell me what happened."

She leaned her head back against the wooden swing beneath his outstretched arm. She sighed, then spoke in a low monotone. "I met Steve the first night I arrived in Tucson to start a new job. He was an attorney, very successful, very good-looking. We hit it off right away, and before I knew it we were living together. One night, a few months later, we were out having a few drinks, and this friend of Steve's stopped by our table and asked us when we were going to get married. 'Well, what's wrong with right now?' Steve said. I don't know when I've ever been so excited. I loved him, I really loved him, and I knew, then, that he loved me. He grabbed my hand and we got in his car and drove all the way to Las Vegas. We got married at one of those little chapels at two in the morning...you know the kind, where you pay twenty-five dollars and a justice of the peace reads a few well-memorized words, and his wife stands by in her bathrobe and curlers, smiling and yawning and wishing you luck.''

She paused for a deep trembling breath and pressed her palms together, bringing them up against her lips. ''Anyway, things were just fine for about six months, but then I lost my job. I applied at every station in Tucson but no one would hire me. Finally I got an offer from a station in Detroit. He didn't want to move, so....''

''You left,'' Kyle said softly.

She nodded. When had he taken her hand? She couldn't remember. But she realized he was holding it now, gently massaging her knuckles with his thumb.

''We tried to keep the marriage together. We visited back and forth on weekends every two weeks. Every penny we earned went to the airlines or the phone company. It worked out fine for several months, but then he missed a visit. Then another. He started having all kinds of excuses why he couldn't come, why I shouldn't come see him. Business problems. This and that. Finally I discovered he was seeing someone else. I didn't blame him. I was lonely, too. But he called me one night ... didn't even have the decency to tell me in person. He wanted to marry her. He wanted a divorce.''

''When you first left ... were you still in love with him?''

''Yes. Very much. But not enough to give up my career.''

''He should never have expected that of you. He should have been willing to move with you.''

''That's easy to say, but his career wasn't as mobile as mine. He was only licensed to practice law in Arizona. He'd built up a clientele. How could he leave? When it comes down to it, one person in a marriage has to be willing to move, to sacrifice their career if need be, for the other. And I don't think that's fair to either one of them.'' Which is why I can never marry again, she wanted to say. But somehow she couldn't bring herself to voice the words.

His arms tightened suddenly around her. ''I think when two people love each other enough, no matter what, they can always find a way to be together.''

''It's not always so simple.''

"It can be." He stroked her back and shoulders as he hugged her, while rocking the swing back and forth. She clung to him desperately and buried her face against his neck.

"I don't want to go through that again," she whispered, knowing at the same time she couldn't bear to let him go. "I'm not strong enough. It took years for my heart to knit itself back together, for me to realize I could survive on my own."

His lips moved over her shoulder, her neck, and she felt herself succumbing to his magic touch. "Desiree, I want you. I need you. You were hurt badly, I know, and I'm sorry. But you've got to let go of the past. What happened to you before isn't going to happen to us. It's not going to be easy...nothing worth having ever is. But we can't throw it away. Not before we've even tried."

He drew back and cradled her face in his hands. "Give us time, sweetheart. Give us a chance to make things work."

Her eyes brimming with tears, she slid her hands around his neck and pressed her lips against his. His kiss was a warm sure force. She felt his strength pouring into her body, filling her, making her new. Maybe, just maybe she was wrong. Maybe, somehow, they could make things work. At the moment she couldn't imagine how, but what did it matter? How could she possibly say goodbye to him, even if she wanted to?

"Sign here, please." The burly deliveryman extended a clipboard and Desiree dutifully signed her name.

It was Tuesday morning. Kyle had left before sunrise the day before, and Desiree spent the day and night reliving their long weekend over and over in her mind, her body still tingling from the memory of his touch. He called her at the station Monday afternoon, and again late at night when neither of them could sleep. They'd teased and tantalized each other over the phone with vivid descriptions of what they'd be doing if they were together. It had taken hours to fall asleep.

"You'd better let me carry this in for you," the deliveryman said. "It's pretty heavy."

A good five minutes later she finally managed to pry open the top of the large heavy carton. Panting, she turned it to its side, pulled out the contents and stood it upright on the hardwood floor. A chair. A delicately carved mahogany chair with a straight back and powder-blue floral tapestry seat, the kind that would be at home in a long line of matching chairs in an elegant eighteenth-century dining room.

She loved it on sight. The smooth grain was stained a deep reddish color, the same shade as her china cabinet, the same shade as his hair. He must have seen it in an antique shop and known how much she'd like it. What a unique gift! How thoughtful! She ran her fingers along the highly polished rung across the back, touched to her very soul.

That afternoon the hot line flashed in her control room at the station. Her heart leapt when she heard his voice.

"Hi, sweetheart. Miss me?"

"Yes! Oh, Kyle, the chair...it arrived this morning. How did you ever get it here so fast? I don't know how to—"

"You like it?"

"Love it! It's exquisite. Thank you."

"You're welcome. I wanted to make sure you liked it before I send the other one."

"The other one?"

"Sure. You can't just have one chair, for God's sake. It's a matched set or nothing." He chuckled. "Listen, I've got to run. I only had a minute between meetings. See you Friday night, right? Let's eat in. Can you cook?"

"What?"

"I asked if you can cook. The only thing I've eaten made by your two hands is a freshly squeezed orange and a salad."

She laughed. "I can cook."

"Great. I'm dying for a home-cooked meal. Wear something sexy. I'll see you at the airport. Bye."

She smiled at the phone long after he'd hung up. "He's crazy," she muttered to herself. "Absolutely crazy."

Hope your great-grandmother would have liked this. Love, Kyle.

It took three-quarters of an hour for the two deliverymen to set up the new dining-room table and five additional chairs Friday morning. Opened to its full oblong size with the three accompanying leaves, the gleaming mahogany table stretched nearly wall-to-wall across the room. Everything about the table reminded her of Kyle. Its strength. Its beauty. Its polished sophistication. She knew she shouldn't accept such an expensive gift, but she couldn't send it back, either. It blended perfectly with her other furniture and suited the house as if made for it.

No wonder he wanted to eat in tonight, she thought with a grin as she frosted a dark chocolate layer cake later that morning. She popped a leg of lamb into the oven—his favorite food, he'd told her, lobster not withstanding—and set the timer to start baking at four o'clock. After closing the table to a small oval, she covered it with an old-fashioned white lace tablecloth and set out her best china.

When she picked him up at the airport after work, they flew into each other's arms as if separated five months instead of only five days. The aroma of succulent roast lamb assailed their nostrils when they opened her front door, and he closed his eyes, savoring the delicious scent. When they finished eating, he proclaimed it the best meal he'd ever tasted, and promptly whisked the chef off to bed to show his appreciation.

The nights were long with loving, the days warm and fun-filled and far too short. Each morning they exercised and jogged. On Saturday they toured the immense *Queen Mary* and Howard Hughes's *Spruce Goose*, docked at San Pedro harbor. They wandered through the quaint Cape Cod-style harborside shops at Ports of Call Village, where Kyle bought her handwoven Irish linen tablecloths to fit the table in two different sizes. They had dinner aboard the elegant *Princess Louise*, a cruise ship turned restaurant, and toasted a passing tugboat with raised glasses of icy champagne. Sunday they rented bikes and rode along the meandering paths at a large tree-shaded park a few miles from her house, then returned home with sunburned shoulders and noses. They made love in the hushed stillness of early evening, the setting sun glowing on their bodies through the open bedroom windows.

"I'm hungry," she said later, as they lay face-to-face on the plush Persian carpet in her living room, each wearing nothing but a smile. "I feel like I haven't eaten in four days." The brass table lamps on either side of her couch cast a warm glow on the single frosty glass of iced tea they sipped through separate straws.

"It's no wonder, after all the strenuous activity we've had this weekend," he said.

"Are you referring to daytime activity or nighttime?"

"Take your pick."

She laughed. "How many calories do you think we burned up last night? I should go check my scale. I've probably lost five pounds by now."

"Don't get too excited. You're going to gain it all back at dinner. What I have in mind is sinfully fattening." He kissed her on the lips, then jumped to his feet and disappeared into the kitchen.

"There's nothing decent in the refrigerator, unless you want leftover leg of lamb. We ate everything else for breakfast."

"I know," he called from the other room. "We're going to order something in."

"Great!" A sudden craving seized her and her mouth began to water. *A thick Sicilian-style pizza just oozing with sauce and cheese, smothered with . . .* She frowned, shook her head. No way. Not his style. A man who serves pâté and champagne and chocolate mousse on a beach picnic, who orders *canard à l'orange* and escargots in their native tongue, will not go for a gooey rubbery everything-on-it pizza.

He returned with the thick Yellow Pages. Kneeling down beside her, he opened the book on the coffee table and flipped through the pages. "Is there a place around here that makes a good juicy pizza with a thick crust, smothered with mushrooms, sausage, olives, bell peppers, shrimp. . . ." At her astonished expression he said, "What's wrong? Don't you like pizza?" His eyes narrowed and he wagged his index finger at her. "It's un-American not to like pizza."

She burst out laughing and threw her arms around his neck. "I adore pizza! I was afraid to admit it. I thought you only liked gourmet food."

"There's a time and a place for gourmet food, and a time and a place for junk food."

"How profound!" She kissed him, still laughing. "Want to hear a secret? I'm a closet junk-food junkie."

His arms glided around her waist. "Really? A chocoholic and a junk-food junkie? What a woman. I'm impressed. What's your favorite?"

"My favorite what?" Her hands combed adoringly through the silky short hair at the back of his neck.

"Junk food."

"Oh!" Her lips followed the movements of her fingers. "A Big Mac, of course. They put the greatest sauce on those things .... A Big Mac, hot salty fries and a chocolate shake."

She spread kisses down his neck, across his shoulder. His breath hissed in through his teeth.

"That's your favorite?"

"Yes . . . no, wait," she murmured. "Big Macs are my second favorite. My first favorite are S'mores. How I used to love those. Haven't had one in years."

He pulled her more closely to him. "S'mores?"

"Haven't you heard of them?" She settled against him, loving the feel of his strong arms around her, the warmth of his skin. "They call them that because they're so good, you always want S'more. We used to make them on girl scout camping trips." His mouth and tongue paid an inordinate amount of attention to the soft skin behind her ear, and she gasped, arched her neck, closed her eyes. "You . . . toast marshmallows over the campfire until they're hot and gooey, then squish them between two graham crackers and a square of chocolate. The . . . hot marshmallow makes the chocolate melt. . . ." She melted heaving a deep ragged sigh. "It's heavenly."

"I'll bet." He cradled her back over his arm as his mouth charted a fiery trail down her neck to the valley between her breasts. "I'll have to try it some day."

"What's . . . your favorite?" she murmured throatily.

His hand slid up the outside of her thigh, then swept over the curve of her hip to cup her bare breast. "Chicken. I always like a nice juicy . . . breast."

"Do you?" she whispered.

"Yes." His lips closed around the object of his affection and he lowered her to the soft carpet.

"Wait, Kyle . . . the pizza. You . . . you have to order the pizza."

"Later." He spread her thighs apart with his own and covered her with his warm hard body. "Right now," he whispered huskily, "I want S'more."

Before sunrise Monday morning he sat on the edge of her bed, dressed in a dark blue three-piece suit and kissed her goodbye.

"I wish you'd let me take you to the airport," she said as she held him fiercely against her naked chest.

"There's no point. You'd only be stuck in morning traffic." He kissed her again, then stood up. "I've got a busy week of negotiations coming up. I may not have time to call every night."

"Okay."

"I'll miss you."

"I'll miss you." She couldn't stop the tears that trickled down her cheeks. Damn! She didn't want to cry every time he left, didn't want him to see her this way.

He leaned down and kissed her again, holding her closely. "I need you, Desiree," he whispered. She watched him go through a blur of tears.

It was the longest week of her life. She bought a stack of cards at a stationery store and sent one each morning. Tuesday she sent him a cuddly stuffed toy lobster of plush red velour, as big as a bread box, which she found in a children's boutique. I'm hungry for you, her note read. She didn't hear from him all day. When she tried calling him at the office, his secretary said he was tied up in meetings, and he didn't return her call.

Wednesday she had a mixed flower arrangement sent to his office, with a note saying, Let's do business together. She called him that afternoon, but their conversation was cut short soon after he thanked her for the flowers.

"I'm sorry I haven't called, honey," he explained. "I've been wining and dining clients all week. I'm in the middle of negotiations for an important contract and I just don't have time to talk."

She sat on the edge of her bed Thursday night, fresh from a shower, about to apply Passion Pink polish to the second to last toenail, when the phone rang. She jumped to her feet and grabbed the receiver, the nail-polish brush still in her hand.

"Hi, lover." The deep vibrant voice never ceased to send delicious shivers up her spine.

She smiled radiantly into the receiver. "Hi. I miss you. I can't wait to see you tomorrow."

"I miss you, too. And thanks for the stuffed lobster. Didn't do a thing for my appetite, but he's cute." He paused. "Listen, Desiree. I've got bad news."

Her stomach tensed. The radiant smile disappeared. "What's wrong?"

"I expected these negotiations to wrap up today, or by noon tomorrow at the latest, in time for me to catch my flight. But there's no way that's going to happen. The client refuses to budge on his price, and I'm not going to give this thing away. We need at least three, maybe four more days. They've got a bunch of guys here from Cleveland who don't want to fly home for the weekend and come right back. We've agreed to work Saturday and Sunday to get this thing done."

She sank onto the bed. A hot flash of disappointment coursed through her, touching every limb, every nerve. She tried to stab the nail-polish brush back into the mouth of the tiny bottle, missed and stabbed again. The bottle tipped over and rolled off the nightstand, trailing Passion Pink polish along the hardwood floor into the bathroom. Tears of hurt and frustration burned behind her eyes. "Damn!"

"I'm sorry, sweetheart. The last thing I wanted was to spend the weekend locked up in a conference room, haggling with a bunch of cigar-smoking men. But I have no choice. I'd like to turn it over to my negotiating team, but I've got two new people and I can't afford any screw-ups. The deal's too important. Please don't be angry."

"I'm not angry." The words shot out sharply, like an expletive. Steve's excuses for not coming to see her were always just as crucial, just as plausible, and always at the last minute. She believed him right up to the bitter end. In the past week apart, did Kyle come to see the futility of their relationship? Was this his way of letting her down softly? No! He was telling the truth.

He had to be! Two tears spilled down her cheeks and she sniffed.

"Hey. Hey," he said softly. "It's only one weekend. I'll be there next Friday, on the same flight I planned to take today. All right? You'll meet me?"

"I'll meet you."

They were silent for a moment. She clutched at one last hope. "What about the manufacturing plant you were looking at down here?" At least if he buys it, she thought, he'll have to fly down here once in a while. "What did you decide?"

"The prospects didn't look good. I decided against it. I'm looking at a company in Tulsa, Oklahoma, instead. I have to fly out there next week."

She stifled a gasp of disappointment. Tulsa. Would he meet another woman there, spend the weekend the way he did with her? Don't be ridiculous, she told herself. He cares for you!

When he spoke again his voice was low, deep, rusty. "Desiree, I miss you. I can't begin to tell you how much. I'm sorry I can't be there tomorrow but I'll make it up to you. I promise."

They said goodbye, and Desiree knelt down, retrieved the half-empty bottle of polish and sat back down on the bed. I promise. How many times had she heard those two words from Steve? Promises were so easily made, so easily broken. She put her feet together, stared at the two unpolished toenails on her left foot, so pale and lifeless next to the eight bright pink half-moons. Why bother to paint the last two? Who would notice?

I believe him. I believe him. She chanted the words over and over throughout the weekend. He does care for you. He will come back. Each time the phone rang she jumped to answer it, disappointment piercing through her with razor sharpness when it wasn't Kyle. She felt like a daisy whose petals were slowly being ripped from her body. *He needs me. He needs me not. He wants me. He wants me not.* You'll see him Friday, she reminded herself. *If he comes.*

Somehow she managed to get through the next day at work, and the next. Her calm voice and brittle smile masked the ache that wrenched at her heart. Wednesday night he still hadn't called. She threw herself down on the bed, closed her eyes and tried vainly to banish from her mind the vivid memories of their weekends together. But the room echoed with remembered laughter, electric touches, softly whispered endearments. She blinked open her eyes, wishing she could make him magically appear in the doorway. The room seemed empty, a lifeless void. Like her heart.

From that moment at Catalina Island when she'd first acknowledged her love for him, the feeling had grown and blossomed until every fiber of her being seemed to shine with newly found sustenance from within. Everything she did now was for him. Every thought, every wish, every deed. She felt she could never again feel happy or whole without his warmth, his caring, his sharing.

Yet she still didn't know if he loved her. She could see affection in his eyes every time he looked at her, feel it in his touch every time they made love. But he'd never said the words. *Did* he love her? Could there be any kind of future for the two of them? Or would it always be like this . . . a few glorious weekends, with long stretches of lonely disappointment in between?

Why? Why? she asked herself silently as she covered her face with her hands. Why did I do this to myself again? Why did I let myself fall so deeply, so hopelessly in love with him, when I knew this would happen?

"And *hopeless* is right," she whispered brokenly. But there was no one to hear.

"When I said I wanted a *hot* and *sizzling* evening," Desiree said into the mike, "I wasn't referring to the temperature outside." She mustered every ounce of vigor inside her to spice up her voice. "Hope the thermometer takes a nose dive in the next hour or so. Right now it's ten minutes before six o'clock on this Thursday afternoon. Coming up is Dave Hamilton and thirty minutes of non-stop music on KICK 102. Catch you tomorrow, same time, same place."

Pulling off the headphones, she stood up and wearily shook her curls. She filled in the broadcast log with all the promos she'd played and did a little end-of-the-day housecleaning in the studio. She cued up an especially-long sentimental love song which matched her mood, then slumped on the stool and toyed with the frayed white edge of her cutoffs. The lyrical feminine voice sang out softly, sadly. She closed her eyes.

> We're on opposite shores, but lover I'm yours,
> Come take me away...
> I'm lost in your arms, fall prey to your charms
> when you hold me that way...

The studio door opened. "Hi," he said softly.

"Kyle." She didn't realize she'd whispered his name aloud, didn't hear the agonized relief in her voice as she jumped off the stool and threw herself into his arms.

Desiree opened her eyes. The room was as empty and dismal as before. She breathed in deeply and shut her eyes again.

He enfolded her in his embrace, capturing her mouth with his.

"I've thought of nothing but you since I left. I could hardly eat. Sleep." He covered her face and neck with kisses. His fingers found the back closure of her bra, snapped it open, swept around and under the flimsy garment to cup her bare breast. His eyes gleamed as they held hers. "I've missed holding you, touching you. I couldn't forget what you feel like. It tormented me, day and night."

A delicious warmth penetrated her body. She hugged her arms to her chest as the soft sweet words of the song swam around her, through her.

> I tremble like a child, a fire burning wild,
> you bring out the woman in me.

His mouth feasted on hers. Their tongues met, skirmished. She closed her eyes, tightened her arms around his neck and swayed against him. He reached down with two hands, undid the snap and zipper of her cutoffs and pulled her down to the floor with him. She gasped, opened her eyes dizzily, but made no move to protest. In a few swift movements he removed the clothing between them, drawing her to him. At his lightest touch she shuddered with desire.

I want you so badly, I love you so madly,
take me now and set me free.

The studio door flew open. "Move over, gorgeous, it's my turn."

Desiree blinked rapidly, refocusing glazed eyes. Dave, the slightly balding deejay on the evening shift, towered above her.

"What were you doing, sleeping?" he asked.

"N-no."

"I'll bet." He cracked a grin. "You've been off in a fog ever since the day that boyfriend of yours showed up in his green Maserati."

"He's not my... boyfriend," she said.

"No?" Dave's voice echoed with surprise. He peered at her, his forehead furrowed. "You didn't break up though, right?"

"Not... exactly."

He shrugged, checked his watch and shook his head in confusion. With an aside glance at the promo log on the counter, he said, "Good thing you've been filling this thing in. Can't afford any mistakes now."

She slid off the stool, grabbed her purse and leaned against the counter, her mind still in a daze. "Why? What do you mean?"

"Didn't you hear the news? Old man Westler's planning to put this place up for sale. Retire."

She snapped back to reality. "For sale! When?"

"Don't know. He hasn't made any announcements yet. It's just a rumor going around."

A wave of fear flooded her body. If the station was sold... new owners were notorious for doing major overhauls, firing everyone and starting over from scratch. She bit her lip. "I was miserable enough without hearing that kind of news, Dave."

"Well, cheer up. It's just a rumor. Time for you to split, now, so git." He sank onto the stool and picked up the headphones. Jerking his thumb over his shoulder, he added, "By the way, there's a surprise waiting for you in the parking lot."

She stared at him blankly. "A surprise? What?"

Dave waved an impatient arm. "Go see for yourself. Go, woman. Get lost!" He flashed her a knowing smile. "I'll give you one little hint. It's not a green Maserati."

Ten

———

Desiree punched open the studio door. A surprise? In the parking lot? If it wasn't Kyle, then who or what could it be? She raced down the hall, through the empty reception area and threw open the double glass doors. The dry heat seared her skin after the cool air-conditioned interior of the station, but she didn't notice. She turned the corner of the building to the asphalt parking lot, then stopped dead in her tracks.

Parked across and in front of her car and three others, a sleek white Cadillac stretch limousine gleamed in the late afternoon sun. A tall dark-haired man in a uniform stood beside it, his hand resting on the back door handle.

"Ohh!" she cried aloud. What did Kyle do? Send a limo to take her to the airport, so she'd fly up to see him? She couldn't go! It was only Thursday. She had to work tomorrow.

She took a few tentative steps forward.

"Miss Saint Germaine?" the man asked.

She nodded. He opened the door, gestured for her to step inside.

The hell with it, she decided. Be spontaneous. Respond to the moment!

She flew to the door, bent down and slid inside onto a plush burgundy velour seat. Suddenly long arms scooped her up, drew her against a broad chest, and warm familiar lips came down on hers.

Desiree's eyes opened wide with surprise and met Kyle's twinkling green ones. She let out a moan of pleasure as her arms came up around his neck. Vaguely she heard the car door shut, another door open, and the motor start as Kyle hooked a hand under her legs, lifted her across his lap and settled her bottom between his thighs.

"What are you doing here, you crazy man?" she whispered against his lips.

"I couldn't wait until tomorrow." His mouth rained kisses across her cheeks. "I couldn't stay away another day."

They kissed long and deeply, holding each other tightly, drinking of each other as if dying of thirst. The car moved forward. She ran her hands across his wide shoulders, his back, his ribs, reacquainted herself with each hard familiar muscle, bone and sinew.

"I missed you," she whispered when she was able. "God, I missed you. I thought I'd die."

His arms roved over her body, under her snug-fitting T-shirt, to glide up the smooth soft flesh of her back. "I'm sorry I wasn't here for the weekend. I'm sorry I haven't called. I came straight from Tulsa. I've been there all week, negotiating a major contract. I barely had time to eat and sleep."

"Tulsa? Oh, Kyle. I'm so glad you're here." She hugged him. Hard. "I'm sorry if I sounded angry that night on the phone. I was just so disappointed. I wanted you so much."

"I know. I wanted you, too." He kissed her again, cuddled her against him.

"How long can you stay?"

"Only tonight."

She tilted her head back, mouth opening in dismay. His reddish-brown hair was brushed back from his forehead in neat waves, and he looked even more handsome than she remembered. "You flew down here for just one night?"

He nodded. "I left the negotiations to the rest of the team this afternoon. Looks like things will wrap tomorrow in Tulsa, so I'm heading back to Seattle first thing in the morning."

She sighed sadly, then leaned her head on his shoulder, wrapping her arms around his chest. "I won't think about it right now. I'm going to enjoy every precious minute we've got."

She took a moment to glance about the interior of the car. Wide deep plush seats faced each other across an expanse of wine-colored carpet. A small television was built into the textured leather wall on one side, along with a stereo receiver and CB radio. Above it, a tiny bar held a row of crystal glasses engraved with the Cadillac logo. A phone hung on the opposite wall, beside a magazine rack. The green neck of a bottle poked out from an ice bucket at their feet.

"This is incredible," she breathed, then turned to kiss him. "You remembered what I said that night, didn't you? About the limo?"

He grinned. "I did."

She glanced down at her denim cutoffs and the lavender T-shirt that hugged her curves, silk-screened with the KICK logo in black and silver. "I feel terribly underdressed. If I'd known I was going to ride in a limousine I would have worn my electric-blue silk dress."

"You mean the one that's—"

"Open in the back, cut just off the shoulder, terribly chic," they sang out in unison. It had become a standing joke with them, and they laughed.

"Don't worry. For what we're about to do, you're dressed perfectly."

For the first time she noticed he wasn't wearing his usual three-piece suit. Instead, he'd dressed casually, in a cream-colored polo shirt that showed off his tan and blue jeans that fit like old friends—still deep denim-blue, but snug across the hips, whitewashed at the seams and pocket edges. His running shoes looked well-worn, white fading into gray.

Her eyes narrowed curiously. "Where are we going?"

"You'll see. This night is for you." He squeezed her hand. "You're going to see all your fantasies come true. First, a stop at your favorite restaurant."

There were three or four elegant restaurants in the area that she was particularly fond of, but she didn't remember specifying a favorite. Since he refused to elaborate she sank back into the plush seat with a resigned sigh and enjoyed the ride. A few minutes later the limousine pulled up to a McDonald's restaurant and parked in front of the door.

"You've got to be kidding!" she squealed, nudging him in the ribs with her elbow. "A limo to take us to McDonald's?"

The driver stepped to her side of the car, opened the door and helped her out. Once inside, Kyle ordered five Big Macs, three large orders of french fries and a chocolate shake.

"Someone's joining us?" she asked.

A smile twitched his mouth. "No, it's just the two of us. You did say these were your favorite?"

She nodded her head with helpless laughter. "I did."

"Good. I don't want you to go hungry. Anything else?"

"No, thank you," she said. "This'll do just fine."

A pleasant-looking man with silvery hair stepped in through the door, accompanied by a woman of about the same age. They both looked over their shoulders. "Whose do you think it is?" he whispered, gesturing with his head toward the waiting limousine.

The woman searched the faces in the crowded room with awe as they stepped behind Kyle and Desiree in line. "I don't know. I don't recognize anyone. Seems funny to see it here. Maybe—"

"Look no further." Kyle put his arm around Desiree and faced the couple with a charming smile. "No famous faces here tonight, folks, just a famous voice. This is Desiree Saint Germaine, from KICK-FM."

Desiree felt her knees grow weak. Famous voice? She wanted to sink into the floor and disappear. But to her surprise and relief the man's eyes widened with apparent admiration.

"No kidding? You're Desiree?" The man clapped his hands together. "Well, what do you know. I listen to you all the time!"

"So do I," said the woman at his side, who was now beaming with delight. "And so does our son. He especially loves your show."

Desiree's face lit up with a genuine smile and she instinctively held out her hand. "Thank you. I...I always like to meet my listeners."

The man shook her hand with enthusiasm and introduced himself and his wife. "I'm honored to meet you. Really honored. Wait until Ron hears about this!" He grabbed a napkin from the dispenser on the counter and pulled a pen out of his pocket. "Would you autograph this for m—for my son, please?"

Desiree laughed. "Sure." She wrote "Life's a KICK at 102 FM" and signed her name. The couple were clearly thrilled. Several other people came forward and clamored for her autograph. It seemed as if she'd signed twenty napkins, paper bags and placemats when Kyle finally grabbed her arm and steered her out the door with their bags of food.

She leaned back against the seat, laughing, as the car pulled away. "I can't believe you told them who I was!"

"Why? You're a celebrity. Don't tell me no one's asked for your autograph before."

"Only a few times. I told you, people don't recognize me by just my voice. And I don't go around introducing myself so brazenly, the way you did."

"Why not? You should. It'd be great publicity."

Where had she heard that before? Barbara. The day the woman from some restaurant called and asked her to emcee their opening party. Suddenly she wanted to do the party, lots of parties, wanted to get out and meet the people who made her job possible.

"I feel so fantastic when you're here," she cried, throwing her arms around his neck. "You make me feel young and beautiful and desirable and talented."

His eyes shone with tender admiration. "Only because you are."

The driver took them to the mile-wide tree-shaded park where they'd ridden bicycles two weeks before. Kyle handed the McDonald's bags to Desiree. He pulled a bulky canvas bag out of the trunk, threw the strap over his shoulder and grabbed the ice bucket. "We'll be back in a while," he said to the driver.

"Hope you brought a good book to read." The driver chuckled and signaled goodbye with a courteous wave.

Kyle put his arm around Desiree and gave her a squeeze. "Follow me."

The sun hung low in the sky, bathing the lush green lawns on either side of the bike path in warm golden light. They followed the path until it curved about a small lake, and climbed up a short hillside to a grassy knoll. He stopped beside a picnic table and set down the canvas bag. A cement fire ring stood in a clearing a few yards away.

Kyle pulled out a red plaid blanket and shook it open. "I hope you like dining alfresco. This spot was crucial for phase two of my little plan for the evening."

"Phase two?" Desiree said, give him a curious look as she took an end of the blanket.

"You'll see."

She laughed and helped him spread the blanket on the grass. "Well, if your Picnic in the Park is anything like your Day at the Beach, I'll *really* be impressed."

"Oh yeah?" He straightened and crossed to her side, grinning.

"You're a master of creativity when it comes to picnics. Not to mention other out-of-door . . . activities."

Laughing huskily, he put his arms around her and drew her close. She met the warm look in his eyes and felt her throat constrict with an overpowering rush of affection.

"It's been a long two weeks, hasn't it?" he whispered.

"It seemed like two years." Her heart pounded as his lips nuzzled the hair curling softly at the side of her neck. She hesitated a moment, wanting to melt against him, to wrap her arms around his neck. She felt a desperate need to tell him how much he meant to her. *Kyle, I love you,* she wanted to say. But was this the right time? Would he feel pressured to admit to the same depth of feeling, or think she expected some sort of commitment in return? Before she could speak his mouth came to hers in a quick urgent kiss and he withdrew.

"Let's eat while it's still lukewarm," he said gruffly. He grabbed the bags of food and sat down on the blanket.

Desiree had to take a deep breath to stem the tide of tears that stung her eyes. She dropped down beside him and crossed her legs, managing a smile. "Right. Let's eat."

The sun had descended below the treetops and the sky had turned a pale dusky grey by the time they finished the milkshakes, consumed two hamburgers each and most of the french fries. Several yards below them a flock of ducks gathered at the water's edge, bobbing about expectantly.

"Throw them a hamburger," Kyle suggested.

Desiree laughed, plucked off the top bun from the remaining burger and scrambled down the shore incline. Kyle followed. They ripped the bun into small pieces and tossed them into the water near the shore.

"Here, little quackers," she cried. The ducks made grateful noises as they darted toward the food. When she'd flung them the last piece, she raised her palms. "Sorry. All gone."

Disappointed, the ducks turned tail and glided away across the silent water. Kyle took Desiree's hand in his and led her back up the slope. "Come on. Main course is finished. Leftovers dutifully disposed of. Now, for dessert."

He transferred the canvas bag to the hard ground beside the fire ring. After drawing out several small logs from the bag, he arranged them in a pile inside the cement ring on top of the paper trash from their dinner.

"Why a campfire?" she asked, kneeling down beside him.

Casting her a mischievous grin, he lit the fire and fanned it to life with an empty styrofoam carton. All at once she realized what he must be up to and she drew an astonished breath.

"S'mores?" she cried. "But how—"

"Phase two of Your Fantasies Come True." Kyle dug out several additional items from the canvas bag, placed each one in her arms with a flourish. "One bag of marshmallows. One box of honey graham crackers. One extra large bar of chocolate. And two specially modified coat hangers."

She laughed her delight and would have hugged him if her arms hadn't been full. "How did you ever remember the ingredients?"

His eyes twinkled. "I didn't. But I have five sisters, remember? It seems a loyal girl scout never forgets how to make a S'more."

A refreshing summer breeze blew across the lake, cooling the evening air. They sat close together on the hard-packed earth, toasting handfuls of marshmallows to a golden brown over the glowing embers. She showed him how to squeeze the hot marshmallow and chocolate between two graham crackers. When he pressed the crackers too hard, she leaned forward and licked the molten white goo that squeezed out the sides. They laughed, kissed, passed the sweet confection back and forth until their hands were sticky and their faces streaked with charcoal.

"Happy?" Kyle asked when they'd consumed as much as they could stand. Darkness was fast approaching now. The park was lit only by the last rays of sunlight and the glow of a few well-spaced pole lamps. "Feel indecently indulged?"

"Yes," she sighed contentedly.

He chuckled. "Good. Time now to indulge one of my fantasies." He brought her back to the blanket and pulled her down beside him. "Sipping Perrier Jouet in the park at sunset with the girl of my dreams."

He withdrew a champagne glass from the ice bucket and the slender green bottle, then proceeded to open it. Large, delicate white flowers were hand painted on the dark green grass. Desiree knew an expensive bottle of champagne when she saw one. "Wow, this must be a special occasion."

"It is. It's the three week anniversary of the day we met." He filled the glass and lifted it to her lips. She sipped.

"Mmmmm. Delicious."

He brought the glass to his own lips and drank. Their eyes met and never wavered as they passed the glass back and forth, slowly finishing the tangy bubbling wine. Her heartbeat performed an erratic dance and she felt, all at once, enveloped in tenderness; it seemed as if her very soul would melt under the endearing affection she saw glowing in his eyes. He set the glass aside, and murmuring her name, he collected her in his arms and sealed her mouth with his.

Warmth spread through her body like wildfire as she wrapped her arms around him, answering his kiss with all the fevered urgency in her heart. They sank down on the blanket and rolled to their sides, clinging together, mouth against mouth, tongue meeting tongue, her softness molding against his hard strength. His hands roamed down her back, over her buttocks, then up again to her shoulders as her hands tangled in his silky hair.

She swallowed his kisses like nectar, each kiss alternately filling her and increasing her thirst until she felt limp with desire. She lost pace with her breath, her blood spinning through veins that seemed delighted to swell and pump. Through the layers of their clothes she felt the heat of his body and of his desire, and that part of her which sought him throbbed in joyous response.

He left her mouth to scatter hot open kisses across her cheek, along her jaw to the softness of her throat. His chest moved in rapid sync against hers, and she felt his breath, moist and fragrant against her ear. When at last he spoke, his voice was deep and rusty, caressing in its warm intensity.

"Desiree, I love you."

Tears welled in her eyes. She wound her arms around his back and held him to her, wanting to heighten their contact, to prolong it for all eternity. "I love you, too, my darling," she whispered.

He rolled with her to his back and kissed her again, long and lovingly, his hands stroking her hair. "Desiree . . . if you only knew how much I've longed to hear those words from you. I started falling in love with you the night we met. The very first night."

"So did I," she murmured against his lips. "I've wanted to tell you for such a long time, but I was afraid—"

"Afraid?" He smoothed the hair back from her forehead. "That I didn't feel as strongly about you as you did about me?"

She nodded. A tear spilled from her eye to trickle down her cheek as she saw his answering nod and knew he'd harbored the same fears.

"It seems we've been holding back our feelings to no purpose." He smiled warmly, tracing a fingertip across her lips. "But there's nothing to stop me from saying it now. I love you, Desiree. With all my heart. I love you."

A radiant smile curved her lips and she pressed her mouth against his in a soft kiss. "I love you," she whispered. "I love you. I love you. I love you!" She punctuated each tender admission with a kiss at the corners of his lips, on his chin, his nose, his eyes, his forehead. She rested her cheek against his, slowly drew it across the scratchy pull of his day's growth of beard, then covered the roughened skin with small kisses.

A deep and abiding affection thrilled through every fiber of her being, filling her with such joy that she couldn't help laughing out loud. He hugged her to him, laughing in return. It felt so good to have him here, so wonderful to be in his arms, so right to be able to show her love this way.

"Desiree, I need you," he said, cradling her face in his hands and bringing his lips to hers for one more deep urgent kiss. He rolled her to her back and cupped one of her hands in his. Bringing her fingers to his lips, he gazed down at her, his eyes a mirror of the love she felt shining within her own.

"I don't want to leave you, ever again," he said. "Not even for a day. I want to share the rest of my life with you, to have you by my side, with me always. Will you move to Seattle with me and be my wife? Will you marry me?"

Eleven

———

Ten seconds dragged by as Desiree lay still beneath him, her mind a whirl of conflicting emotions. She felt astonished, flattered and thrilled, all at the same time. She wanted to jump to her feet, grab his hands and shout, I love you! Of course I'll marry you! But on the heels of her initial joy came despair, wrenching at her heart, keeping her earthbound. How could she possibly move to Seattle? How could she marry him?

"I . . . don't know," she said finally as she reached up to caress his cheek. "I love you. More than I'll ever love anyone. And I would love to be married to you. But . . ."

She sighed, then rolled out from under him and sat up, curling her legs under her Indian-style. "Kyle, you have to understand how important my career is to me. I've—"

"Desiree," he cut in, "your career—"

"Wait," she said. "Let me finish. Let me explain. I've wanted to perform on radio since my seventh birthday, when my grandpa gave me my first transistor radio. I used to lie awake at night, dreaming up the things I'd say and do. My voice is my biggest asset. The personality I've created on radio is an important part of me. And I have definite goals for myself. I don't intend to stay a deejay forever. I'd like to do a cartoon voice, voice-overs for commercials, other promotional work. Southern California's the best market for that. And in five years, maybe ten, I hope to manage a station somewhere."

She twisted her hands in her lap, raising her eyes to his in a plea for understanding. "Radio is my life, a living breathing part of me. I couldn't give it up."

Kyle sat up and grasped both her hands earnestly in his. "Desiree, I respect your talent and your goals. I admire you. Don't you realize that? Your career means as much to me as it does to you. I'd never want you to give it up. Never."

"But I'd have to if I married you."

"Why? Why can't you have both marriage and a career?"

"Because . . . well, for one thing, we live and work over a thousand miles apart!"

"We do now, but . . ." He grasped her hand in his, brought it to his lips, kissed each knuckle in turn. "I thought . . . I know this is a lot to ask, since you're doing so well here. You have fans . . . boy do you have fans!" He grinned and glanced heavenward, and she knew he was thinking of the scene earlier in McDonald's. "But a talent like yours would be welcome anywhere. I'm sure you could find a job in Seattle. Any decent station would snap you up, especially after the rave reviews you've gotten lately in the newspaper."

She shook her head. "It's not that easy. Good jobs like mine are hard to find, especially for women."

"You'll never know if you don't try, will you?"

She chewed her lower lip pensively. "I am doing well here. The ratings aren't in yet on my new show but I've gotten stacks of mail, and I know Sam is pleased with my work. This morning I would have said my job's guaranteed for at least another year. But . . ." She sighed. "I'm not so sure now."

"Why? What happened?"

"I just heard the station's up for sale. The owner, Adam Westler, bought the place as sort of a hobby a few years back. He made his money years ago in something else. Oil, I think. If he sells out, there's no telling what will happen to me or anyone else at KICK. The new owner might not be so keen on female deejays. I could be out of a job in two seconds.''

A broad grin spread across Kyle's face. "Great! Then you'd have no reason to stay down here!"

Desiree batted his arm playfully. "Hey, I'm talking about being fired! Whose side are you on?"

"Our side. I want us to be together, and anything that'll help make it possible is good news to me. I say, look for another job fast, before the station changes hands. You'll get a far better offer from another station if you have a good job behind you."

"I doubt it'll make any difference. Wages are tops here. Seattle's a small market. There's no way any station up there could come close to matching my salary."

"Who gives a damn about salary? I make more money than we can ever spend. I'm talking about the job, the drive-time shift you want so badly."

"It'd be nothing short of a miracle if I was offered a drive-time shift in Seattle. I've never even been there! I don't know anyone in the business."

"But I do."

"You do?"

He nodded. "I've done some heavy radio advertising for Sparkle Light in the past year." He laid her hand across his thigh and stroked it with gentle fingers. "I've been thinking about this for the past few weeks. I . . . hope you don't mind. I know you could have done it on your own, but I thought if I set something up, it would move things along that much faster. I took the liberty of making a few phone calls."

Her eyebrows shot up. "And?"

"Ed Alder, the program director at KXTR in Seattle, is on the lookout for some new talent. He'd like to meet you. Do you have an audition tape?"

"Yes. It's about a year old, but still pretty good."

"Would you like me to deliver it to him? Do you want to fly up for an interview?"

"I . . . I suppose I could—"

"Fantastic!" He drew her to her feet, squeezed her hands excitedly. "I'll give you the grand tour of Seattle. You'll love it, I promise! I'll even set up a dinner at my parents' house. You can meet my family. I've told them all about you. They're dying to meet you."

"Your family? Oh, no!" she laughed. "This is sounding more and more official by the minute!"

"It is official." His arms encircled her waist and he kissed her soundly. "How soon can you get away? Can you fly back with me tomorrow morning?"

"Tomorrow morning?" She laughed, caught up in his enthusiasm. Even if she did find a job in Seattle, how long would it last? How long before she would have to leave, move to another town? *Don't think about that now,* she told herself. *Catch your moments of happiness while you can.* She coiled her arms around his neck, eyes glowing with love for him.

"I have to work tomorrow. But I'm free for the weekend. I could take the evening flight. Can you set up an interview for Sunday?"

He hugged her fiercely close. "You bet I can."

"Two dozen?" Desiree cried with delight as Kyle placed the enormous bouquet of red roses in her arms. The modern Seattle airport terminal still bustled with activity as she stepped off the plane at ten-thirty Friday evening.

"You shouldn't spoil me like this. Three roses the day after we met. And now two dozen at the airport. What's it going to be next time? *Three* dozen?"

"Definitely." His arms closed around her hard and strong, crushing the flowers between them. "Every bride should carry three dozen red roses in her bridal bouquet."

She smiled against his lips. "Don't go jumping to conclusions, Mr. Harrison. I agreed to meet you for the weekend, but I *didn't* say I'd marry you."

"You will, my beautiful lady." His lips meshed with hers in a searing kiss. "You will."

Through the wide plate-glass windows in the terminal, Desiree caught a glimpse of tall dark pine trees silhouetted against the black sky. It seemed both strange and wonderful to see a city airport surrounded by pines, instead of palms.

"I see you have a thing about Maseratis," she said a short time later, after Kyle had loaded her small bag in the trunk of his silver sportscar and spun out onto the highway.

He nodded, grinning, as he shifted the Maserati into high gear and zoomed around slower traffic. "The only way to drive. I've managed to get ahold of one of these beauties every time I've flow into L.A., but I'm not always so lucky. You should have seen the crate I got stuck with all week in Tulsa." When he described the problems he'd encountered with his rented four-door sedan, Desiree's shoulders shook and her eyes watered with helpless laughter.

A short drive took them to an elegant condominium complex in a lovely wooded area outside of town. The Tudor-style brick and stucco buildings, enhanced with dark wood trim, seemed to sprout up from the depths of a dense pine forest.

"I feel like we're up in the mountains!" Desiree stepped out of his garage and breathed in the heady scent of the surrounding pines. "I can't believe you have places like this so close to the city."

"A few more minutes down the freeway, and we'd have really been out in the countryside. You'd love it in winter. You can reach deep snow in practically no time." He unlocked the heavy oak front door and led her inside, flipping on light switches ahead of them.

Desiree took a step down into the spacious sunken living room. Her shoes sank into the thick champagne-colored carpet as she looked around her with awe. Books of every size and description and a myriad of art objects filled floor-to-ceiling teak shelves on two sides of the room, along with an elaborate stereo system, speakers, television and video tape recorder. Colorful modern prints hung over the long blue-grey sofa and Danish teak end tables. Track lighting illuminated the room from beams in the sloped vaulted ceiling. There was a brick fireplace, a built-in wet bar, and a long dark-blue tile counter that passed through into an immaculate modern kitchen with gleaming wood cabinets.

"It's beautiful, Kyle."

He dropped her suitcase by the door, then caught her hand in his. "It is now that *you're* here. Come on. Let me show you the rest." In addition to the living room and kitchen, the condo boasted three cheerfully decorated bedrooms and bathrooms, a large master suite, a laundry room, garage, and a small fenced yard.

"I love it!" Desiree said as Kyle rested her suitcase on a low teak table in a corner of his bedroom. "But I have a confession to make. When you mentioned your house in Seattle, I never imagined a condominium. Somehow I expected to find an enormous mansion on five acres, complete with circular drive and sixteen servants."

He pulled her into his arms. "A man on his own doesn't need a big fancy house to rattle around in. This complex was a far better investment."

"You own the whole complex?" she asked in surprise, and then laughed. "I should have guessed!"

"After we're married, it'll be different. We'll build the biggest most elaborate house money can buy."

"We will?"

"Yes." His mouth traveled up her neck, nibbled at the soft skin behind her ear. "We'll get an architect to design the place to complement all your beautiful old furniture." His breath was a warm moist vapor against her ear as his fingers brushed the sides of her breasts, then slipped around to the buttons on the front of her blouse. "We'll get rid of my modern stuff, if you want. Build a huge formal dining room for your new table." He opened first one button, then another. "Music room. Game room. Office. Country kitchen. A giant master suite complete with sauna and Jacuzzi bathtub, built around an indoor garden." He pulled apart the soft fabric and reached around to unsnap her bra. Then, with one hand splayed across the small of her back, he reached under the loosened bra to cup her breast in his hand. "And five bedrooms. No, six."

"S-six?" Her head fell back as she arched against him.

"Sure. One guest room, and one for each kid."

She gasped, as much from the effect of his nimble fingers as from his startling declaration. "Five children?"

"Well, that's negotiable." He laughed, slid his arms around her bare midriff and hugged her tightly against him. "I enjoyed growing up in a big family, always wanted one myself."

Suddenly he drew back slightly, his voice deeply serious. "You do want children, don't you?"

She nodded. "Very much. I don't know about five, but two or three at least." She felt his chest contract as he breathed a sigh of relief.

"As many as you want. And we'll hire a nanny and a cook and a maid to take care of them while we're working."

"Sounds perfect. Almost too perfect. I think I'd be afraid of a life filled with so much . . . perfection."

"We can do it, Desiree," he said softly. "Together, we can do anything."

They smiled into each other's eyes for a time, and she felt as if time had crystallized around them, sealed them in a safe sweet vault, where happiness was guaranteed to those who loved and hoped and worked hard and dreamed the same dreams.

"I always wished I had a twin sister," she said at last. "My mother used to console me by saying I'd grow up and have twins of my own one day."

"In that case you're in luck. Twins run in my family." His eyes danced mischievously as his lips came down to brush hers. "And I can't think of anything I'd enjoy more than making children with you."

"Oh, no! It's raining!" Desiree cried when she looked out the bedroom window the next morning. A light drizzle fell from a gloomy grey sky.

"So what's new?" Kyle opened his closet and pulled out a pair of jeans. "A little rain won't stop us from sightseeing. I've got plenty of umbrellas. And I'll make you a dollar bet it stops by noon."

She shook her head, tossing a pair of shorts and a few summer blouses onto a nearby chair as she rummaged through her suitcase. Thank goodness she'd decided to pack jeans and a long-sleeved shirt after all. She hadn't even thought of bringing a raincoat. Who needed a raincoat in summer?

"You're willing to risk a whole *dollar*?" she said, laughing. "What faith!"

"It's my father's favorite saying. Every time he makes a dollar bet on something, he wins."

"*Every* time?" Desiree sat down on the edge of the bed to put on her sandals, changed her mind and pulled on socks and tennis shoes instead. "This I've got to see. For a dollar, you're on."

By ten the sky had cleared to a brilliant cloudless blue. "I told you," Kyle grinned as they hopped into his car and headed for the wharf.

"I'm a believer," she said, laughing. "I can't wait to meet your father. He sounds like a real character."

A weekend didn't leave much time for sightseeing, especially with a family dinner to attend that night and an interview at KXTR on Sunday afternoon, but Kyle seemed determined to squeeze in as many sights as possible in the time allowed.

"Seattle was the last stop for prospectors rushing north to the Klondike in the gold rush of 1898," Kyle explained as they walked hand in hand through the shops at Pier 70, a nineteenth century wooden steamship pier. They climbed the steep pedestrian staircase to Pike Place Market, a noisy colorful profusion of sidewalk stalls overflowing with country produce, flowers and seafood, then walked back down to the waterfront on Alaskan Way.

While Kyle waited for their take-out lunch of shrimp and clams, Desiree ducked inside a T-shirt shop and ordered a bright green shirt for Kyle stamped with the slogan, THIS SHIRT IS GREEN.

"I'll get you for this," he laughed when she presented him with the gift. He dragged her to the water's edge, threatened to dunk her in the harbor, then drew her close against his chest instead. "Take that," he said, kissing her. "And that. And that." Despite the public place, despite the streaming fries and seafood growing cold on a nearby bench, the punishment continued for quite some time.

Desiree loved the city. She loved the blending of old and new, the rustic waterfront and charming curiosity shops against the backdrop of modern skyscrapers just blocks away. She loved the crisp clean air and the tall green pines sprouting here and there and the blue blue sky, more vivid and clear than any sky she'd ever seen. She was fascinated by the native Indian and

Eskimo crafts, the folklore and the totem poles, the nearness to Alaska and the woodsy carefree atmosphere that seemed to pervade the area. *We're not at work, we're at day camp!* the people of Seattle seemed to say.

At a curio shop, she bought an Eskimo rock carving of a huge bear devouring a wiggling fish. "It's a symbol of strength and power," she explained as they made their way back to the car. "Perfect for your desk at the office. Which, by the way, is the sight I'd like to see next."

"Which office? The one at Harrison Engineering, in Auburn? Standard Tool and Die, in Tacoma? Sparkle Light in St. Louis? Or maybe you'd rather see—"

"Stop showing off!" She poked him in the ribs. "I want to see your main office, in downtown Seattle."

A few minutes drive along city streets brought them to the tall high-rise building that housed Harrison Industries headquarters on its top floor.

"I've only got a handful of people here to help keep an eye on things," Kyle explained as he gave her a swift tour of the simple suite of offices. Like his condominium, the furnishings and decor were modern and tasteful, a cheerful splash of color against stark white walls. "The important part of this corporation are the individual companies themselves. They only consult me for an occasional problem or an important negotiation. Mainly, I sit up here and run interference."

"What a view!" Desiree said breathlessly as he led her into his office, a large airy room with a solid wall of windows overlooking the downtown area and Elliot Bay beyond. She stopped beside his wide desk, which was ringed with framed photographs of numerous grinning babies, grade school children and five stunning young women. "Who are *they*?" she asked, indicating the women's pictures with a nod of her head.

"The kids? My nieces and nephews." His arms came from behind her, grasped the edge of the desk and pinned her in between. "Or were you referring to all these gorgeous sexy women?"

She cast him a shrewd suspicious look over her shoulder. "Well? Who are they?"

"Jealous?" He laughed, pulled her back against him, and said in a low voice, "They're my sisters." His hands crossed over her tiny waist, then glided up to capture her breasts. "So you see, you have nothing to worry about."

"I see," she whispered huskily as she closed her eyes and rested her head back against his chest.

"But I'm going to have something to worry about if we don't get out of here in a hurry," he murmured against her ear. "Unless you want me to make love to you right here on the floor of my office."

"We can't. We'll be late. Your parents are expecting us for dinner at six. We have to go home and change."

"True. We'd—" To her surprise she felt him stiffen behind her. His arm flashed out and grabbed a memo slip beside his phone. "This must have come in after I left last night." He picked up the phone and rapidly punched a series of numbers. "I'll just be a minute."

Desiree moved to the windows, rested a shoulder next to the side wall and drank in the view.

"Rand?" she heard Kyle say behind her. "What time did you get in? How'd things go?"

The sun gleamed on the windows of the city buildings below, which stretched out toward a sparkling blue bay. Wouldn't I love to have a view like this every day, she thought, instead of the bleak beige walls of my studio.

"What?" Kyle cried. "You gave up our entire negotiating position. We can't break even on the contract now!"

Desiree glanced at Kyle in alarm. He was leaning against the desk, one hand gripping the phone to his ear, the other curled into a tight ball at his side.

"Don't give me that," he said. "You knew where to call me. And I was back in the office yesterday at noon. Dammit, you gave the thing away, Rand!" He barked out a few cutting observations and slammed down the phone. "Come on, let's get out of here." He wheeled toward the door.

Desiree followed, her stomach knotting with anxiety. What had happened? Kyle barely glanced in her direction as they rode down the elevator and drove back to his condo. When he'd unlocked the front door and ushered her inside, she finally drew the courage to ask him what was wrong.

"What's wrong?" he muttered, stalking across the living room and down the hall. "I'll tell you what's wrong. Because I left Tulsa early to see you, because I left the negotiations in the hands of a bungling idiot, Standard Tool and Die just lost over a hundred thousand dollars."

She gasped in dismay. "A hundred thousand! Why?"

Kyle stopped in the doorway to his bedroom and faced her. "The client put the pressure on while I was gone. Rand panicked. He lowered the price, gave away every cent of profit on the contract."

"Oh, Kyle. I'm so *sorry*." She put her hands on his waist and raised agonized eyes to his, but he broke both hand and eye contact with a swift turn and a deprecating wave of his hand.

"It's not the money. It's the *principle* of the thing. Two hundred people will be busting their butts to meet a deadline, and for what? We won't make a dime. We don't need busy work. What a *waste*." He strode furiously into the room. "If I'd stayed and finished the job myself…damn! Rand ought to know what he's doing by now. If you can't trust your—"

He uttered a sharp curse and stumbled, then bent down to pick up something from the floor. A white leather sandal. Her sandal. He whirled on her, holding the shoe aloft with rigid arms. "Damn it, Desiree, don't you ever put anything away? You've been here less than twenty-four hours and already the place looks like a pigsty!"

His icy glare sent a cold wave of trepidation down her spine. Her eyes darted around the almost immaculate room for evidence of her misbehavior. Her suitcase and vanity bag stood open on a low table. A few items of her clothing lay on the bed and a nearby chair. A glass of water sat on the nightstand. Her other sandal lay smack-dab in the middle of the floor. But that was it. Not perfectly in order; hardly a pigsty.

Her temper flared at his unjust accusation. "I'm sorry, Kyle, if I'm not neat enough for you," she said, her voice clear and even. "In future, I'll try to—"

His muttered curse silenced her. She winced as he picked up the second sandal, gathered up her scattered clothing and threw it all into the suitcase.

"We've got fifteen minutes to get dressed," he hurled at her over his shoulder as he banged open the bathroom door. "I'm going to take a shower. Join me if you want."

"Don't count on it!" she shouted.

"Suit yourself!" He slammed the door.

Desiree sank down onto the bed, heart pounding in fury. Could this really be the same bed where they made slow luxurious love that morning? Could this be the same man who'd held her so tenderly in his arms, whispered words of love, pleaded with her to be his wife?

She knew his anger stemmed not from a misplaced shoe but from the news of his negotiation gone wrong. And that was what hurt the most. If he hadn't left Tulsa a day early to see her, he'd have finished the negotiations himself and, no doubt would have gotten the client to give up every penny of that hundred thousand dollars, and more. She'd made him feel guilty for breaking their weekend date, and he'd ignored his obligations to appease her. If anyone was to blame for his company's loss, it was she.

She'd told him a long-distance relationship would be fraught with problems. Still, she hadn't expected anything so serious to happen, or so soon. Already she'd become a major thorn in his side.

She unbuttoned her blouse, folded it and the other clothes Kyle had thrown and placed them into her suitcase. Taking her outfit for the evening out of Kyle's closet, she sat back down on the bed and clutched the hangers to her chest.

What timing, she thought. A family dinner. She had to go; it would be rude to back out at this point. But Kyle was barely speaking to her. How on earth would she get through it? Smile, she told herself. Be charming. Ask all the right questions, tell a few jokes, have yourself a great time. Don't let them see you're hurting. And leave. Tomorrow. On the first plane.

Twelve

———

You said this was going to be a small family dinner."

"It is. Just a few close relatives."

They'd finished dressing with a minimum of conversation and driven to a quiet residential area on the north side of town. She'd tried to tell him again how sorry she was. Sorry about his company's loss; sorry it had soured things between them. His answer had been a silent shrug. What more could she say?

Kyle parked at the curb near a charming two-story red brick house, and helped Desiree out of the car. She counted seven other cars, mostly large sedans and station wagons, crowding the curb and driveway.

"How many relatives is a few?"

Kyle barely glanced at her before heading briskly up the curving red brick walkway. "Count your blessings; my oldest sister and her four kids moved to Des Moines last year." His clipped tone managed to make the words sound cutting, demeaning.

She tried to ignore the anger rising in her chest and concentrated instead on the heady fragrance of the rose bushes blooming vibrantly on either side of the path. Neat hedges and colorful flower beds surrounded a verdant green lawn, and she noticed a long wooden swing, similar to the one she had at home, hanging from the porch rafters. The front door stood open behind an aging screen door, and she could hear laughing voices and bustling activity inside.

She fingered the combs covered with tiny seashells that pulled her hair back from her face. It seemed hard to believe Kyle had just bought them for her on their carefree expedition that afternoon. The fluted scooped neckline of her silky midnight-blue blouse was embroidered in the same color with flowers in a cut-away design, and she wore steel-grey slacks and matching grey pumps. She'd packed the outfit with such high hopes, wanting to make a good impression on Kyle's parents.

"I hope I look all right," she said. Not that it mattered.

Kyle stepped up onto the porch without a backward glance. "You look fine."

"How would you know?" Desiree scoffed. "You haven't looked at me once since you stepped out of the shower."

He turned and threw an arm across her shoulder, pulling her roughly against him. His voice sounded low and harsh against her ear. "Look, let's try and be civil to each other tonight, shall we? Keep a leash on your temper until we get back home."

Keep a leash on her temper? She pressed her lips together to prevent the sarcastic retort that formed in her mind. She'd be damned if she'd let him see how deeply his anger affected her. It was her last night with Kyle, her last night in Seattle. She'd act like she was having a good time if it killed her.

At that moment a young boy pressed his nose against the screen, stared out at them, then darted away. "Hey, Mom, Kyle's here with his girlfriend!" a shrill voice cried.

Before they could move a petite attractive brunette pushed open the screen door. Desiree recognized her from one of the pictures on Kyle's desk.

"Finally! We were starting to think you two had skipped town on us!" The young woman beamed, stepped out and squeezed Desiree's hands warmly. "It's Desiree, right? I'm so glad to meet you! I'm Linda, Kyle's sister." Desiree couldn't help returning the woman's friendly smile. Linda turned and gave her brother a big bear hug. "It's about time you brought someone home to meet the family, you big lug. Mom's been in a positive tizzy. She's been cooking all day. Now come on in," she said to Desiree, taking her hand. "Everyone's dying to meet you."

Desiree took a deep breath as she walked inside, mentally preparing herself for an evening of difficult role-playing. She'd avoided crowds and promotional events during her radio career, and her childhood, spent in a big rambling house with only one brother and a pair of reclusive parents, had in no way prepared her for the hubbub of a big family gathering. And a big family gathering it was. In quick succession she was introduced to four friendly beautiful sisters, three brothers-in-law with hearty handshakes, more than half a dozen giggling and gurgling nieces and nephews, an elderly aunt, a bachelor uncle, two Siamese cats and a bouncing golden retriever.

To her surprise, however, Desiree found herself responding almost immediately to their infectious enthusiasm. Everyone seemed delighted to meet her and strove to make her feel welcome. Soon she was laughing and returning spontaneous hugs and kisses, matching quip with quip, bantering freely as she did on the air.

"Pay close attention, now," said Joanna, a beautiful redhead, after she and her identical twin had introduced themselves. "There'll be a quiz on names and birth dates after dinner!"

"I'll never pass!" Desiree laughed.

A tall blond man with a thick mustache, husband to one of the twins, gave Desiree a particularly ardent welcoming kiss, then punched Kyle on the back. "Way to go, buddy," he cried, winking.

For the first time since they'd arrived, Desiree caught Kyle's eye. A flicker of emotion crossed his face, something like admiration mingled with regret. She felt a stirring within her and she smiled hesitantly, hopefully. He started to take a step toward her when a cheerful voice rang out above the party hum.

"There you are!" A rosy-cheeked wisp of a woman in a blue dress and flowered apron squeezed through the crowd and laid a hand on Desiree's shoulder. Her short dark-brown hair was streaked with grey, and the deep laugh lines around her mouth and pale-blue eyes promised a sunny personality. "I'm Stephanie, Kyle's mother. I'm so delighted you could come."

Desiree knew at once she would like her. As she thanked Stephanie for inviting her, Desiree's heart swelled with gratitude for the welcome she'd received and regret that she may never see these lovely people again.

"I'm sorry the place is such a zoo," Stephanie said. "I warned the girls to at least leave a few of the kids at home, but they all insisted on coming."

"I'm glad!" Desiree said. "In a family this size it's better to just jump right in and meet everybody at once."

"Brave girl you've got here," Stephanie told Kyle. She encased Desiree in a hug, then tilted her lips up toward Kyle for a kiss. He leaned down and gave her a smack, then threw an arm over her shoulder.

"You look beautiful as always, Mom. Is that leg of lamb I smell?"

Stephanie Harrison looked first at her son and then at Desiree, a quiet smile on her lips. "What else would I make for my favorite son but his favorite meal?"

He chuckled and gave his mother an affectionate squeeze. At the same time his eyes met and found Desiree's. She read there a silent apology, a plea for a truce, for forgiveness. Her heart turned over. More than anything, she realized, she'd love to be a part of this happy exuberant family. She didn't know if it would ever happen, but just for tonight she wanted to pretend it would. She wanted to rush into Kyle's arms, tell him all was forgiven. She settled for an answering smile that spoke of her love and granted him unconditional amnesty.

He heaved a deep sigh of relief, wrapped his other arm around Desiree and pulled her close to his side. When he lowered his head to whisper against her ear, his voice was rife with emotion. "If we slip down the hall to the back room for a few minutes, do you think anyone will notice?"

Before she could reply, a glass door slid open at the back of the living room. "Hey, why didn't someone tell me they were here?"

Desiree jumped, startled. If Kyle hadn't been standing next to her, she would have sworn the voice she'd heard was his. She turned around and caught her breath. The man crossing the room could only be Kyle's father. Except for the facial lines etched by time in this man's handsome tanned face, and the silvery hair threaded thickly among the red and brown, the resemblance between the two was uncanny. He possessed Kyle's trim powerful build, the same brilliant green eyes, the same high cheekbones and slightly upturned nose. She felt as if she'd been granted a vision of how youthful and attractive Kyle would still appear in years to come.

"Well, well. Hello and welcome," he said, enfolding Desiree's hand in both of his. "I'm Dan, the old man of the house."

"Old man, nothing!" Desiree heard herself say. Laughter shouted out around her.

"I knew I was going to like her!" Dan grinned as he put his arm around Desiree. "Say, has anybody given you a tour of this place yet? No? Well, then, come on!"

She flashed Kyle an apologetic glance as she was led away. He hid a smile and telegraphed a return message of frustrated longing. A small crowd of youngsters tagged along behind as Dan showed Desiree around the house. She felt overwhelmed by the sense of warmth and love of family that they seemed to radiate throughout. Pictures of Kyle, his sisters and the grandchildren hung everywhere, together with framed awards and countless childish but clearly cherished attempts at pottery, weaving, watercolor and fingerpainting. The children proudly pointed out their own particular works of art, and Desiree praised their efforts. Dan had an amusing anecdote for nearly all of the rooms, which were stuffed with odds and ends of furniture, some new, some old, as if he and his wife couldn't bear to throw anything out. The general clutter made her feel right at home. At least his parents aren't neat freaks, she thought with a smile.

"Soup's on!" Stephanie cried. Dan led her back to the dining room and rang a loud brass gong hanging beside the kitchen door. The children scrambled out to the back porch, where a picnic table had been set for them. An arm darted out from the general uproar and to her relief and delight Desiree found herself nestled in Kyle's arms, against his chest.

"I think there's something to be said for small families after all," he growled. "Whose idea was it to come here, anyway?"

She tipped her head back and smiled at the love she saw reflected in his eyes. "Yours," she said. "And it was one of your better ideas. I love your family."

He kissed her, long and hard. Around them she heard good-natured hoots and catcalls.

"Hey, cut out the mushy stuff!" a voice cried.

"Save it for Christmas, under the mistletoe!"

They pulled apart, laughing.

Desiree took a seat next to Kyle at one end of the long lace-draped dining-room table. Throughout the delicious meal, she was beseiged with friendly questions about herself and her work. She heard countless Harrison family stories and shot back with a few tales of her own, which were met with uproarious and appreciative laughter.

"Kyle offered to buy us a big new house after he started doing so well," Stephanie confided, leaning across the table toward Desiree. "And you know what I said? I said, thank you, but no thank you. I raised six children in this house. It was big enough then, and it's big enough now. And if you think I'm going to pack all those pictures and knickknacks and whatnots to move somewhere else, you've got another guess coming!"

"Grandpa! Grandpa! Guess what?" A small girl in pigtails raced into the room and climbed onto her grandfather's lap. "I passed the Polliwog test at swim lessons and next week I'll be a Frog!"

"Wonderful, sweetheart." Daniel kissed the freckled cheek. "Keep up the good work. Maybe you'll make the high school swim team someday."

"High school, nothing," said the girl's father. "Someday she'll make the Olympic swim team."

Daniel slapped the tabletop. "Damn right! Excuse me, Stephanie. Say, who wants to make a dollar bet Tracy makes it to the Olympics?" Wallets flashed and several dollar bills were flung on the table amid general laughter and applause.

"You wait and see," Kyle told Desiree with a knowing wink "She'll make it." By the time the peach and apricot pies were brought out for dessert, Desiree felt as if she'd been a part of this fun-loving family for years. After coffee, adults and children alike spilled out onto the front driveway, where Kyle's father pulled out a box of fireworks left from the family Fourth of July party the week before. The children raced around the yard, drawing designs in the darkness with blazing sparklers. Everyone clapped in delight as screaming rockets sailed through the air and fire fountains gushed red white and blue up to the night sky. Caught up in the excitement of the celebration, Desiree waved sparklers and shouted her delight along with the rest of them.

All too soon the evening came to an end. Dishes were done, goodbyes said, and families piled into individual cars for the drive home. "I hope we'll be seeing you again very soon, and often," Stephenie said as she hugged Desiree goodbye on the front porch.

"You will, Mom." Kyle said, wrapping his arms around Desiree.

"Who wants to make a dollar bet we dance at their wedding before the summer's over?" Daniel asked, a twinkle in his eye.

"It's a bet." Kyle whipped a dollar out of his pocket and shook his father's hand with gusto.

A warm glow started in the pit of Desiree's stomach and spread to the tips of her fingers and toes. Every time my dad makes a dollar bet, he wins, Kyle had said. If things worked out at the radio station tomorrow, if they offered her a job, maybe, just maybe...

"Have a good time?" Kyle asked a few minutes later, after they'd climbed into his car and were speeding down the highway.

"I had a great time. Your family's wonderful. Every one of them."

"Ah! But then you haven't met my pigeon-toed Aunt Bernice from Boston, who lives in an attic, wears Shakespearean costumes and paints moody abstracts of dancing flamingos in tutus."

"Sounds to me like she'd fit right in."

He playfully punched her thigh, and they both laughed. "Hey, woman, come here." He extended his arms across her shoulders, pulling her against him as he drove with his left hand. "I've been dying for a moment alone with you all night. I wanted to apologize for acting like a complete jerk this afternoon. God, I could kick myself for the things I said."

"It's all right, sweetheart." Sliding her right hand up across his chest, she caressed his neck. "I know why you were angry. A hundred-thousand-dollar loss is no laughing matter. And it's my fault that—"

"No, it's not. None of it was your fault. Leaving Tulsa early was my own decision, and I had no right to take my anger out on you. Harrison Industries isn't going to collapse over one lousy contract. And Kyle Harrison won't collapse if a few shoes are strewn around his bedroom." He kissed the top of her head and massaged her neck through her silky mane of hair. "Do you forgive me?" he asked hoarsely.

"I forgive you," she said. "Just tell me you love me."

"I love you, my darling," he whispered against her hair. "I love you." Her hand slipped down to caress his thigh. Slowly. Lovingly.

"Be careful what you touch down there," he strangled out, "if you want me to get us home in one piece."

"Getting a *piece* is exactly what I had in mind," she said with a wicked grin.

"Your skin is silky soft. Smooth. Like baby skin. So sexy." His soapy hands traveled across her slim shoulders, over her firm rounded breasts, down the sleek incline of her waist.

"I like the way you feel." She ran her fingers over his slippery wet biceps. "So hard and firm. Like iron."

The moment they'd gotten home, they'd come together in a mad frolicking frenzy right there on the thick plush carpet before the front door.

"You're wet," he'd said, smoothing his fingertips across the perspiration which had beaded her brow. "What do you say we go check out the deco tile in my shower?"

"That depends," she'd said with a mischievous grin. "Is it a co-ed shower?"

"Is there any other kind?"

Now, inside the over-sized shower stall with its clear glass door and gleaming blue and white tile, Desiree grabbed the bar of scented soap and stood on tiptoe to wash Kyle's shoulders and lather the hair across his chest. Her massaging fingers followed the bubbles which slid down the V-shaped wedge of hair and past his navel.

"Better... watch it," he cautioned, taking a sharp breath, "unless you want to be dragged out of this shower before we get a chance to rinse off."

"You wouldn't." Her eyes flashed a teasing challenge as she straightened up and pulled him against her. She rubbed the soft bar of soap across the small of his back, down his buttocks to the back of his thighs. "Think of the trail of hot soapy water we'd leave across that beautiful carpet all the way to the bedroom."

"Yes. Think of it." He grabbed her around the waist and reached for the shower door handle, but she wriggled out of his grasp and jumped back under the shower's warm spray.

"Wait!" She raised her fists in a fighter's stance and glared at him. Water ricocheted off her head and shoulders in a fine spray and soapy rivulets drifted down her breasts to her abdomen. "It's your fault I got all hot and sweaty and I'm not leaving this shower until I'm finished."

He laughed, then took another bar of soap from the ceramic soap dish and built up a frothy lather in his hands. "All right. I concede. As long as I'm allowed the honors of finishing." He knelt down before her and began to soap her calves with long loving strokes. She didn't protest. When his soapy fingers reached up to tantalize her thighs, she grasped his shoulders for support and a gentle sigh escaped her lips. He slid his arms around her waist then kissed his way up over her stomach, finally pausing to sip the warm water streaming down the smooth narrow valley between her breasts.

"You're one beautiful woman, Desiree." He ran his tongue around the lower perimeter of one breast, then up to flick back and forth across its taut pink crest.

"Oh, Kyle..." Her fingers twined in his silken wet hair, pulling him still closer against her. "Do you have any idea what that does to me?"

In answer he stood up and crushed her mouth against his. She could feel his surging desire pinned between them like a shaft of steel. "The same thing it does to me, my love," he said thickly. Taking a ragged breath, he leaned back against the shower wall, worshiping the length of her body with his eyes, reaffirming how much he loved every plane and hollow and curve. A flame kindled deep within her and her eyes brimmed over in response. He lifted her to him.

"Kyle...?" she said, more with surprise than hesitation. She wrapped her arms around his neck as he held her suspended in his embrace.

"You said," he intoned hoarsely, "that you wouldn't leave until you were... finished."

"That's right. I... did." She lowered herself onto him, sheathing him with her loving warmth. He filled the space inside her, which ached with need for him, filled her to her very soul. "And you have a remarkable technique for... consummation."

His fingers dug into the firm flesh of her thighs as he held himself within her and sealed his mouth to hers. She could feel the tension building within him, a mirror of her own turbulent passion. Their tongues moved in an erotic mating dance, keeping pace with the movement of their bodies, which rapidly increased in force and intensity. Heat pulsed through her veins, a fire that couldn't be quenched by the water spraying against their fevered skin.

"I love you, my darling," she whispered against his lips. "I'll always love you."

"And I love you." His lips met hers again, and they rocked, bodies fused together, with a rhythm as ageless as the sea. And then, together, they hurtled off the edge of the earth.

Much later, they lay in bed facing each other, heads cushioned by the same pillow, arms and legs entwined in the darkness. His fingers toyed gently with damp strands of her hair.

"Marry me, Desiree," he said softly.

"I want to, Kyle," she whispered. "You know that. But even if I manage to get a job in Seattle, even if everything works out the way we want . . . do you really think you can put up with someone like me forever? I'm not the neatest person in the world."

"I'll put up with you any way I can get you," he said, lovingly stroking the curve of her neck. "You did me proud tonight. My family adored you, just as I knew they would."

She snuggled up against him, rested her head on his shoulder and sighed. "I wish you could meet my family. They'd love you, too. But my brother's in Denver now. My parents moved to Florida after they retired. I can't take any more time off, and to get any of them to come out West before Christmas would take an act of God."

"Or a wedding."

She trailed her fingers along his muscular arm, then looked up to meet his gaze through the darkness. The hunger she saw there caused her heart to pump wildly. "Or a wedding," she echoed softly.

Thirteen

———

It's *definitely* going to rain." Kyle took a seat opposite Desiree at the small table next to the window. Despite foreboding weather, they'd spent the morning touring the Pacific Science Center and decided to have lunch at the elegant revolving restaurant atop the 605-foot Space Needle.

Desiree leaned close to the glass, admiring the panoramic view of the city and surrounding lakes, bays and mountains. "It's breathtaking!" she cried, then frowned at the gathering dark clouds that seemed to close in on them with astonishing speed. "I just wish the sun would stay out for more than five minutes at a time."

"We've still got at least an hour of sunshine," Kyle said, with the certainty of a man who's lived in a rainy climate all his life. "And since the restaurant makes one full rotation every hour, you'll get to see the whole view by then."

The spinach salads and fresh broiled salmon were delicious. When the dessert cart stopped by, Desiree shook her head decisively.

"Are you sure?" Kyle raised a skeptical eyebrow, then turned to glance at the mouth-watering array. Chocolate mousse pie. Strawberry tart. Cheesecake smothered in cherries.

"I'm *sure*." Desiree squeezed her eyes shut. "I've been splurging far too often since I met you. Please, don't tempt me."

Kyle laughed. "What a tower of strength. Far be it from me to try to sway a lady to my way of thinking once she's made up her mind."

"I'll remind you of that," Desiree said, "next time you wake me up in the middle of the night."

"Ahem." He silenced her with an emphatic glare.

Just as they emerged below from the high-speed elevator, the sky opened up. They raced back to the car, huddling together under Kyle's umbrella. Despite the overhead protection, huge drops splashed against Desiree's open-toed shoes and seeped through her panty hose to drizzle down her legs.

"Phew!" She slammed the car door and slumped against her seat. "When it rains here, it really rains!"

"You ain't seen nothing yet. This is just a light sprinkle."

She grimaced. "Wonderful. Heaven help us if we ever get caught in a *real* thunderstorm." She shook the skirt of her navy-blue shirtwaist dress, trying vainly to dry the dark wet spots left by the rain and rubbed her hands briskly over her damp nylons.

Kyle started the engine and pulled out from the curb. "I like the rain. It's soothing. A quiet gentle sound."

"That's great if you're inside looking out," Desiree said. "Or barefoot, or wearing boots." The windshield wipers, she noticed, were fighting a losing battle against the steadily increasing torrent. She glanced in the vanity mirror on the visor and cringed at the wayward tendrils of hair around her face, which had frizzed in the moist air. "Splashing through puddles can be fun. But *not* right before a job interview."

"Don't worry," Kyle said. "They'll expect you to be a little soggy. Everyone's used to it around here."

"Everyone except me. I guess I'll have to get used to it, though, won't I?"

A few minutes later, he parked in front of a tall high-rise building in the center of town, then gave her directions to find the radio station. "Alder and the receptionist came in specially for this appointment. They said the door would be unlocked. I'll wait for you down here." He kissed her. "Good luck, sweetheart."

"Thanks. I may need it." She opened her umbrella against the downpour, then stepped out and hurried up the street to the building's wide glass doors. A quick elevator ride brought her to the top floor. She caught her breath in astonishment when she stepped into the sleek modern lobby with its plush red carpeting and gleaming oak furniture. The KXTR logo and slogan, *Something EXTRA for Seattle*, in shiny gold three-dimensional letters, were mounted on a mirrored wall behind the receptionist's massive desk.

This makes KICK look like a hick station, she thought. Her cheeks flushed as she remembered the black vinyl benches and unpretentious decor of her own station's small lobby. She introduced herself to the receptionist, who buzzed the program director on her phone.

"Mr. Alder will see you now," the young woman said to Desiree. "Please follow me."

She led her past a glass cabinet filled with trophies and awards, down a long hall hung with framed photographs of deejays, and stepped into a room which put the offices at KICK to shame. Textured wallpaper was printed in subtle beige with the logo pattern of the broadcasting company that owned the station. The desk, which dominated the room, was massive and modern. A bar was built into one corner. Leafy potted plants stood regally beside floor-to-ceiling windows, which offered a magnificent if rain-streaked view of the city below.

"Mr. Alder?" the receptionist said. "This is Desiree Saint Germaine."

A ruddy-faced dark-haired man unfolded his incredible length from a swivel chair and extended a large hand to her across the desk. "Miss Saint Germaine. So nice to meet you." His face broke into a wide grin, flashing large white teeth. He spoke with a pronounced Texas twang.

She smiled as his hand gripped hers in a firm handshake. "I'm pleased to meet *you*, Mr. Alder. Thank you for seeing me on a Sunday. I know the station runs seven days a week, but I'm sure you don't usually come in over the weekend."

"No problem, no problem at all. I understand your time constraints. You've got a job to do." His long arm swept toward the leather chair facing his desk. "Please, have a seat." He sat back down and lit a cigarette with a gold lighter.

While she continued to admire the imposing office, he told her the history of the station. She'd done her homework; she knew quite a bit about the station already, but he cited facts about its ratings and advertising rates that further impressed her.

"They stole me away from a top Houston station last year," he said proudly, blowing out a puff of smoke, "and I'm doing my damnedest to make us the highest rated station in the Pacific Northwest." She filled him in with details of her background and experience that weren't listed on her résumé. His cigarette had burned down to a stub when he offered to take her on a tour of the station.

The station was the epitomy of modern sophistication. The newsroom and sales offices were sharp and clean. Production rooms were outfitted with the latest equipment, and the music library was immense and well-organized. He led her past two small empty control rooms, then stopped at the third door where a familiar red beacon flashed just outside.

Desiree looked through the window beside the door into the glass-paneled room. A man sat at an enormous state-of-the-art console, moving his hands animatedly as he spoke into the mike. His deep tones emanated from speakers overhead. She took an excited breath. The equipment was *gorgeous*. Nothing like the antiquated console she worked with at KICK. Her hands fairly itched to touch that board, to move those beautiful levers up and down.

Then her gaze fell on the binder that lay open on the counter before the deejay. *A script!* The stations where she worked had always allowed her to speak extemporaneously; she was free to ad lib and joke as she pleased. She'd never worked from a script before and felt that it would remove the spontaneity and excitement from the job. She bit her lip as disappointment surged through her. *Oh, well, you can get used to anything,* she reminded herself.

"Well, whaddya think?" Ed asked after they'd returned to his office and taken their former seats. "Pretty nice, huh?"

"Very," Desiree said sincerely. "You run a beautiful operation here."

"Well, good. Listen. I heard the tape you sent. I like your voice, and you've got some good experience. Your on-air personality might work for us here." She waited expectantly as he lit another cigarette, sat back in his chair and took a drag. "So, I'd like to offer you a position."

Desiree's heart leapt. Was it going to be so easy?

"But I'll have to be frank with you," he went on in his Texas drawl. "There's no way we can match or even come close to the salary you're earning now. I can offer you twenty-five thousand. That's it."

She frowned. "That's not very tempting. Especially since I'm still employed at KICK."

"I know. In fact, I couldn't understand, at first, why you'd even want to leave a prime market like Southern California to come work for us, at any price. Then Kyle explained something about an upcoming management change. Still not a reason." He took a drag on his cigarette and waved it in a questioning gesture. "Am I right in thinking there's something else behind this career move? Something between you and our businessman friend, maybe? Like wedding bells?"

Desiree felt her cheeks redden. He chuckled. "I see how it is. Well, I guess, then, salary won't really be the deciding factor here," he said. "If you want it, the job's yours."

"Which shift?" Desiree asked uncertainly. "Morning or afternoon?"

Her question seemed to surprise him. He frowned, scratched his head, then stubbed out his cigarette and folded his large hands on the desk. "Let me tell you this straight out," he said, forcing a smile. "We only had one female deejay at KXTR, and she didn't work out too well. I can't be sure how you'll go over, and ratings, you know, are the name of the game. But Kyle Harrison's spent a lot of dollars at this station, and I thought your tape was pretty good, so I'm willing to take a chance on you. But as to the shift—"

Desiree felt the hot rush of color sweep from her cheeks to fan across her forehead. Pretty good? Willing to take a chance? What kind of nonsense was that?

"We can use a voice like yours on nights," he finished.

"Nights?" If he'd slapped her in the face, she couldn't have been more stunned.

"Yes. Two A.M. to 6 A.M.. Five days a week." His white teeth flashed again as he added magnanimously. "With weekends off! How's that sound to you?"

Desiree struggled to keep her voice calm. "Mr. Alder, I worked evenings and nights for seven years. I have the afternoon drive at KICK now. My show receives critical acclaim. When Arbitron comes out with the new ratings, we expect it to be one of the top shows in the area."

"Yes, little lady, but that's Anaheim. People are different down there next to Hol-ly-wood." He emphasized the three syllables of the word with distaste. "No doubt it's quite common to hear the voice of a lovely woman like yourself on the afternoon drive. But let's be frank. You've got a bedroom voice, the kind men want to hear late at night."

A bedroom voice? Desiree shot out of her chair, her heart pumping furiously. "Thank you for your *kind* offer," she spat out, eyes flashing angrily. "I'll certainly think about it and let you know." Then, before he could open his mouth to speak, she grabbed her purse and stalked from the room.

"Damn this rain!" Desiree peeled the clinging damp dress over her head and threw it down in a heap on Kyle's bathroom floor. "Doesn't it ever let up?" In her haste to leave the station, she'd forgotten her umbrella and had been drenched in seconds by the downpour outside.

"Sure. It might be over in a couple of hours." Kyle tossed her a fluffy towel and she vigorously dried her wet hair. "I'm sorry I didn't warn you to bring a raincoat this weekend. It never occurred to me you wouldn't know."

"It never occurred to me to need *any* kind of *coat* in summer!" She stripped off her underclothes, ran the towel over her body and dodged past Kyle's outstretched arm into the bed-room. "Don't you ever find it depressing? Having it rain so much?"

He shrugged. "Sometimes. I guess I've gotten used to it. It seems worth it. It makes everything so green. Don't you ever get tired of all that sunshine back home? Always the same. No change of seasons. No—"

"No!" she fumed. "I *like* it that way. At least it's *predictable*."

Kyle followed her into the bedroom and dropped onto the bed, his eyes never leaving her body as she pulled on a pair of jeans. "Are you sure you want to get dressed?"

"Positive." She drew a pink top over her head and yanked it in place. "Summer's are supposed to be hot. Blue skies and *sun*. I'll take the nice dry climate of Southern California any day over this."

"So would I. Anyone would. But you've got to live where you can make a living."

She whirled on him defiantly. "You're right! And that's exactly what I'm going to do. I'm going to stay in California, at KICK."

He sat up on the edge of the bed and sighed deeply. "Desiree, you have every right to be upset. I'm sorry it didn't work out this afternoon. But it's only one station. There are others. I'll call—"

"No! I'm not going through that kind of embarrassment again. I want the job on my own merit, not as payment for your faithful advertising." She crossed the room to the window, where beating rain blurred the glass in thick rivulets. The dripping pine trees outside stood like sturdy sentinels, oblivious of the downpour. She shook her head.

"I'm sorry, Kyle. I won't work for someone who doesn't respect my talent. And I refuse to take another night shift. You can't imagine what havoc that kind of schedule plays with your life."

"Try another station, then," Kyle repeated. "Even if you get stuck with a night shift, it would only be temporary. I'm certain in a few months, they'd see what they've got, and you'd—"

"You don't know that. I might be stuck doing nights again for years. I won't take a step backward. I paid my dues. I won't do it again!" She took a calming breath then dropped down beside him on the bed, resting a hand on his hard thigh. "Kyle, I love you," she said softly. "You know that. And I do want to marry you. Only—"

His hands shot forward and grabbed hers as their eyes met. "Only what?"

"I don't want to leave Southern California."

He blew out an exasperated sigh, relinquished her hands and crossed his arms over his chest. "Wonderful," he spat out sarcastically.

"Let me explain. When you first suggested I look for a job here, I agreed to give it a try. I almost had myself convinced it would work. But I was wrong. And it's not just the rain, or the rude things Alder said about my voice."

She lay sideways on her bed and absently traced the line of stitching in the blue quilted spread with her index finger. "You have no idea how lucky I am to have made it in Orange County radio. Someday I want to do commercials, TV, film . . . and it's all there. I have a following, a reputation. It's taken me seven long years to get a daytime show. I can't leave just because the station might be sold. I'd be a fool to give up what I've worked so hard for."

He dropped down beside her, his jaw tense, eyes riveted to hers. "You'd be a fool to give up what we have."

"I'm not talking about giving up our relationship. I want to marry you. But I also want to stay at KICK."

"And how do you propose we do that?" he asked sarcastically. "Live in separate cities?"

"Yes!"

He cursed loudly and looked away.

"Look," she went on, "even if we were lucky enough to live in the same city to start off with, there'd be no guarantee we could stay together. I've explained how unstable the radio business is. After a year, maybe two or three at the longest, I'd be out of a job and have to move on."

"Dammit, you're just looking for excuses now! While you're at it, why don't you anticipate every other conceivable thing that could go wrong over the next fifty years?'' He stood up and raked his hand through his hair. "And what makes you so certain you'd have to move on, even if you did lose a job? Who says you couldn't find work at another station in the area?''

"Because a deejay cast adrift is practically untouchable in the same market. You almost always have to move to a new city to find work. Don't ask me why. It's the way this business works.''

He cursed again then strode across the room and braced his arms on the dresser top, his back to her. "So, even if we get married, we can only look forward to seeing each other on weekends and vacations. Twice a month here, twice a month in Anaheim. Or maybe we can buy a house in Portland and meet part way. Is that what you want?'' He shook his head bitterly.

"Why not? As I recall *you're* the one who suggested we meet on weekends. You're the one who said a long-distance relationship could work, not me!''

"That was before I tried it.'' He looked back at her over his shoulder with narrowed eyes. "I can see now why your marriage fell apart.''

She stared at him. "What are you saying?''

"I'm saying you were right. It can't work. At least not for me. I've spent the past few weeks here in body, but not in spirit. And now my business is suffering.''

She swallowed hard, knowing he was referring to the blown contract. Tears threatened and she turned to run, somewhere, anywhere, but he grabbed her arm and caught her to him.

"I love you, Desiree,'' he said urgently. "I don't want to be torn, day after day, between you and my work. I want to be together, live in the same house, share the same bed. I want to spend mornings and evenings with you, make love to you every night, wake up beside you every morning. I want to make a home together, raise children together. We can't do that if we live in separate cities. I want you with me. I want a full-time wife!''

She pulled out of his embrace and took a step back. Her arms fell loosely to her sides. The sound of the rain beating against the windowpane matched the dull thudding of her heart. "I love you, Kyle,'' she said quietly. ''But I can't be the kind of wife you want. Not without giving up my career. And I can't do that. I just *can't!*''

Fourteen

Desiree shivered beneath the old maroon sweatshirt as she trudged barefoot across the damp sand, avoiding scattered masses of dark stringy seaweed. An early morning fog hung low over the Santa Barbara coastline, casting a dull white glow across the bay. She'd walked this beach every morning for eight days now, trying to make some sense out of her life and reason for being. Sam, her boss, had insisted she take the time off.

"You've been stomping around here all week like a ghost with a frozen smile on your face," he'd growled. "Your performance has been smooth. You're the best personality we've got on the air. But something's eating you up inside. One of these days you're gonna break. And I like you too much to sit around and wait for it to happen."

"I'm fine," Desiree had insisted. "Really, I—"

"The hell you are. Look, I'm giving you next week off." He'd waved away her protest with an impatient hand. "Go away somewhere. Relax. Don't tell me where you're going. And don't come back until you've solved your problem, whatever it is. Got it?"

She got it. Santa Barbara, the quiet stately community just up the coast, seemed the ideal place to meditate in solitude. But now, on the Monday morning she was due back at work, she had yet to make peace with herself. She'd checked out of the hotel and knew she ought to get in her car and drive home. But she didn't feel ready. Her heart still ached and tears came to her eyes every time she recalled the Sunday afternoon two weeks ago when she left Seattle.

Kyle had begged her to spend the night, to wait and take her scheduled flight the next morning. But there had seemed no point in staying. Every extra moment she spent with him would only make the ultimate parting even harder to bear.

"I'm sorry," she'd said, throwing clothes into the open suitcase on Kyle's bed.

"Sorry? What good is it to be sorry? Stop packing, dammit!" Kyle had laid a restraining hand on her arm but she'd shrugged it off. "Desiree, don't walk out on me like this. It's pouring rain outside!"

"People are used to rain in Seattle." She'd snapped her suitcase shut with a bitter thud. "It's better if I go now. We've said all we have to say. I'll call a taxi."

"You'll do no such thing!" He'd grabbed the suitcase from her hand. "Look, if you're so set on leaving, I'll drive you to the airport."

"Fine!"

They sat in tense silence as Kyle steered the Maserati over the wet streets. Rain pelted the windshield. When they finally reached the airport, he carried her bag to the counter, waited while she changed her reservation, then walked her to the gate. The flight was just about to board. Desiree fumbled miserably with the shoulder strap on her purse as she purposely avoided his gaze.

"Kyle, I ... I want you to know how much I appreciate everything you've done for me," she said brokenly. "I've felt like a different person since I met you. You've given me more confidence than I've ever had before. I'll always be grateful to you for that." His low muttered curse forced her to raise her eyes to his. The pain which contorted his face hurt her like a physical blow. She bit her lip against an onrush of tears, then raised her hand to cup his cheek. "I hope…can we at least still be friends?"

"Friends?" He grabbed her hand from his cheek, gripped it with angry force for a long moment as he impaled her with his eyes. "Friends? You know that's not enough, Desiree." Without another word he dropped her hand, spun on his heel and disappeared into the crowd.

The day after she returned home, a small box had arrived with a card from Kyle. "I'll always love you, Desiree," the card read. "Like the contents of this white box, we're a perfect matched pair. We belong together. There's got to be a way we can work things out. Please. Come back to me."

A wistful ache wrenched at her heart as she stared at the box. It was pink, not white. Inside, on a bed of pale pink velvet, rested a set of custom-crafted pierced earrings: two delicate golden songbirds, a sparkling diamond chip in each eye.

She'd burst into tears.

The earrings were still in the box, buried under the scarves in her bottom drawer. She'd never wear them. How could she? No more than she could bring herself to wear the pendant again.

The squawk of a seagull yanked her back to the present. She blinked back fresh tears, curling her toes into the damp sand as she walked. She remembered another sea gull's cry on an idyllic afternoon with Kyle at Catalina. Years, not weeks, seemed to have passed since then. The pain of loneliness and loss spread throughout her body until her insides felt like one immense gaping chasm.

Try to remember what life was like before you met him, she told herself as she trudged up the sand, across the parking lot to her car. Did you feel happy? Energetic? Did you look forward to each new day? Yes! You were lonely, but you'd learned to accept it. And you'll have to learn to accept it again.

She opened the car door, cleaned off her feet and got in. Turning the key to auxiliary power, she flipped on the car radio.

"Hope you're having a great morning out there, Santa Barbara," said a cheerful masculine radio voice. "I sure am. On the way in this morning—"

She tuned out the voice, crossed her arms on the steering wheel and wearily lowered her head. Radio. That's where the excitement was. The drama, the thrill, the power she wielded within the confines of her small control room. She'd always loved it. It had been her whole life. Why, then, didn't she care anymore? Where had the magic gone?

"And now for some Streisand," said the radio voice. A pause. And then sweet familiar notes rent the air. Desiree's head flew up and she stared at the radio as if it possessed satanic powers. "Songbird!" Of all the songs to play...

She leaned her head back against the seat and closed her eyes. She knew every note, every word. The lyrics wove through her mind and body, reaching down to her soul. The songbird's sweet music brings others joy, the words said. Her song sets people free. Yet no one knows the songbird. She's sad and alone... lonely. Who will sing for her?

Desiree's chest constricted with an ache of longing, emptiness. I'm nothing more than a voice coming out of a box, she realized with sudden agonizing clarity. I make others happy. But no one sings for me.

You fool, a voice cried within her. He loves you. He's the music in your soul, the one who can set you free. Everything will work out if only you're together. Nothing else matters. Nothing.

She gripped the steering wheel with fierce determination. How could she have been so blind? How could she have imagined she could live without him? Her work meant nothing if she couldn't have him.

She turned on the ignition and stamped on the gas pedal. The engine roared to life. She sped out of the parking lot, down the street, and pulled to a screeching halt in front of the first phone booth she saw.

I only hope I'm not too late, she thought desperately as she jumped out of the car and raced to the phone booth. She dipped into her purse, grabbed her address book and searched for Kyle's office number with trembling fingers. I'll find a job in Seattle, take whatever I can get, she decided. Who cares what shift it is? Who cares what I'm leaving behind? At least we'll be together.

She drummed her fingernails against the booth's glass door as she waited for the operator to put through the credit card call. She'd do her best, she reasoned, make a name for herself, and in no time she'd be on top again. If she lost her job some day and couldn't find another one . . . to hell with it! She'd do something else.

She didn't know what else she would do, couldn't think that far ahead. She only knew she needed Kyle, wanted to spend the rest of her life with him, and her professional future be damned.

"Harrison Industries," an efficient female voice said finally on the other end of the line.

"Kyle Harrison, please." Her voice sounded unnaturally high and shrill in her ears.

"I'm sorry, Mr. Harrison is out of town today. Would you care to leave a message?"

Out of town? Oh God, where was he? In Tulsa again? "Well, I . . . this is Desiree Saint Germaine, and—"

"Oh, yes, Miss Saint Germaine," the woman replied cordially, as if they were old friends. "Mr. Harrison has mentioned you a number of times. How may I help you?"

"I have to talk to him. It's very important. Can you tell me where I can reach him?"

"Certainly. He's in Orange County, California. Would you like the number of his hotel?"

Orange County! Desiree clapped a hand to her mouth in surprise and delight. What was he doing in Orange County? "Yes. Th-thank you very much." She scribbled down the number on the back of an envelope in her purse, then said a hurried goodbye and hung up. Did he come down just to see her? What would he do when he found her gone?

She called the hotel and asked for his room. She let the phone ring a good fifteen times before she slammed down the receiver and glanced at her watch. Nine-fifteen. Damn! Where could he be?

She jumped back into her car and roared off. Thank God she'd missed the morning rush-hour traffic. She could be home in two hours, if she sped all the way and didn't pass any highway patrolmen. He might have stopped at the station and found out she'd be back to work today. Did he hope she'd return home last night? Please, please, wait for me my darling, she prayed silently. I'm coming back to you.

The drive seemed interminable. The car shot past long stretches of dry arid landscape, sped through the San Fernando Valley, over the mountainous Sepulveda Pass, past the L.A. airport, on toward Orange County. At last she turned onto her street, her heart pounding like a locomotive in her breast. Was his car there? Another rented Maserati? Anything? No. The driveway and curb stood empty.

Maybe he came in a taxi, she thought frantically. Maybe he used his key and is waiting inside. She pulled to a halt, raced up to the front door, unlocked it and called his name. The house was hot, musty. As empty as the day she left it.

"Dammit, where are you, Kyle Harrison?" she shouted. Her voice echoed in the stillness.

She called the hotel again. No answer. She called his office in Seattle. "Sorry to bother you again, but I can't seem to reach Kyle…Mr. Harrison at his hotel. Have you any idea where else he might be?"

"Yes. He left word we could reach him at the station this morning. KICK. He—"

"Oh! Of course! Thank you." Desiree hung up, elated. Since she wasn't home, of course he'd wait for her at the station! She peeled off her clothes and took a fast hot shower. Forty-five minutes later she pulled into the parking lot behind the station, dressed in a white denim skirt and a puffed-sleeved pale-blue cotton blouse. She pushed open the double glass doors, disappointment surging through her when she saw the deserted lobby. Only Barbara was in the room, speaking rapidly into the phone behind the wide Formica counter.

"Yes, sir. Fine. I will." Barbara caught Desiree's eye and gestured emphatically for her to wait. "I'll put it in the mail today. Thank you for calling." She disconnected the line and stood up. "Des! At last! You're back." Her eyes gleamed with some indefinable emotion. "How was your vacation?"

"Therapeutic. Listen, has anyone been by here to see—"

"Des, big things have been happening around here while you were gone," Barbara cut in. "Westler's been in meetings all week. And guess what? He sold the station."

"Sold it? When?"

"They just finalized everything this morning. Westler took off, but the new guy stayed around. He said he wants to talk with you as soon as you get in."

"Talk with me?" Desiree asked, stunned. "Why?"

"Don't know. But you'd better hurry. He's been waiting for over an hour." She shooed Desiree off toward the door that led into the station. "Go on. He's in Westler's office."

Frowning, Desiree opened the door and hurried down the hall. What was he going to do? Fire her? She didn't really care. She didn't plan to stay much longer anyway.

The door to Westler's office stood open. She stepped over the threshold, then stopped, frozen. The man behind the desk looked up from a stack of papers, his handsome face grim, unreadable, his green eyes wary.

"Hello, Desiree," Kyle said quietly.

Her mouth flew open, but no words came out. What was he doing, sitting behind Westler's desk? Was this some kind of a joke? Then suddenly, all the jumbled pieces of information she'd learned this morning fell into place in her mind like a reassembled jigsaw puzzle. She gasped in astonishment. "You . . . you *bought the station*?"

He nodded. "Close the door, will you please?"

She complied mechanically. He gestured toward the chair facing his desk. "Have a seat."

She dropped stiffly into the chair, her mind whirling, alternately accepting and rejecting what she'd just heard. Kyle's eyes seemed to search hers for a sign, an indication of her feelings. But she was so taken aback she could only return his stare blankly.

He frowned, then turned his attention back to the papers in his hand. He made a few notations, then set them aside. "I hope you enjoyed your vacation?" The cold brittle edge to his voice cut the air like a knife.

"Yes. It was . . . fine."

"Good." He lifted several sheets from a folder at his left and extended them to her across the desk. She didn't look at them, her eyes still focused on the hard lines of his cheeks and jaw. "It'll take a few weeks before the sale is final," he said. "But in the meantime, you'll be glad to know your future at KICK is secure. You can take over as general manager, or keep your spot on the air, or both. Whatever you like. I've had papers drawn up to make you a partner in the firm. You'll want to take some time to look them over, but what it boils down to is a fifty-percent share after five years if the company shows a consistent profit."

If she felt astonishment before, now she was completely stunned. "Fifty percent share!"

His brief smile ended before it reached her eyes. "Yes. You won't have to worry about job security now." He gave a short laugh. "Of course you'll have a few more responsibilities, but nothing you can't handle."

Tears burned behind her eyes. How could he have thought she'd want the *station*? My God, the idea had never even entered her mind. She didn't even want her job anymore. She wanted him! If only she could fly into his arms, make him understand. She wanted to admit how wrong she'd been, to tell him she loved him and wanted, more than life itself, to marry him. But he was acting so cold, calculating and impersonal.

"I don't know what to say." She swallowed over the lump in her throat. "I never expected you to buy the station. I don't deserve such generosity. Really. I—"

"It wasn't generosity." He stood up abruptly. His eyes impaled hers across the desk. "I had the funds available. I've been looking for an alternate investment for the past month. At the moment this station breaks even at best. But you show outstanding devotion to your work. I'm convinced that, under my direction, with the incentive of partnership, you can turn this place into a real money-maker."

She gasped at his harsh words. He still thought the only thing she cared about was her job. He'd never forgive her for walking out on him, for choosing her career over him. "I . . . see," she strangled out. "Well...I'm sure you'll—" Her voice broke as a sob burst from her throat. Tears streamed down her cheeks. One hand flew up to cover her eyes and she turned blindly, found the door handle and yanked it open.

"Dammit!" Kyle crossed the floor with urgent strides and slammed the door shut then pulled her into his arms. "Are you going to walk out on me again, the way you did two weeks ago?"

She shook her head, his face a blur through a sea of tears. "I don't want to walk out on you, Kyle. But I can't stand it when you look at me that way, as if . . . you hate me."

"*Hate* you? Don't you know by now how much I love you?" Unfamiliar tears shone in his eyes as they held hers. "I'll always love you, Desiree. Good God, what more can I do to prove it to you?"

She sobbed with relief and gripped his back fiercely, her forehead against his chest. "Oh, Kyle, Kyle. I love you, too. I've been so stupid. Can I say now what I've been wanting to shout to the world all day? My career doesn't mean anything to me if I can't have you. Do you still want to marry me? Please say you do. Because I will! I tried to call you this morning in Seattle to tell you, and then at your hotel when—"

"Say that again," he demanded as his hands cradled the back of her head, tilting her face up to his. His eyes began to twinkle in a familiar way and her heart lurched with newfound hope.

"I . . . I tried to call you—" she began distractedly.

"No, no. The first part."

"I said . . . I love you. If you still want me . . . I'll marry you."

"I accept." Their eyes met, each asking the other for forgiveness and receiving it. Then his lips came down on hers in a fiery kiss. His mouth devoured hers, feverishly tasted every sweet crevice, as if to seal their promise by binding them together. She molded herself against him, returning his kiss with unrestrained passion, trying to pour into him all the love she'd been saving, harboring, resisting.

"Has it been as hard for you as it has been for me these past weeks?" he asked hoarsely as his lips slid to her neck.

"Yes. I've never felt so lonely, so miserable. When you sent the earrings . . . they're beautiful, Kyle. I wanted to call, to thank you. But I couldn't. I knew if I heard your voice again, I could never bring myself to say goodbye."

"I longed for you. I reached for you in the night, but you weren't there. When you didn't call, after I sent the earrings, I gave up hope. I knew, then, you were lost to me forever. I thought I'd go out of my mind." He shuddered and hugged her more tightly against him. "I told you, once, that I'd never try to bully you to my way of thinking once you've made a decision. I only bought the station so I'd have an excuse to see you, be with you."

She lifted teasing eyes to his. "Rather drastic measures to take, don't you think? Thank goodness you don't have any stockholders. I could just see you at the next board meeting." She lowered her voice to a stuffy growl. "Who is this broad, Harrison? Is she really worth it? Are you sure she can turn a profit with the place?"

His mouth tilted up in the lopsided grin she'd come to love so well. *"Absolutely."* He kissed her. "With you at the helm, we'll be the top rated station in Orange County in no time."

"No, no, my darling." She shook her head. "I know this sounds ungrateful after all you've done. I never imagined you'd go to such lengths to... God, I can't tell you how sorry I am. But I can't stay here. Not if you're in Seattle." He started to protest, but she raised a finger to his lips. "Please listen, Kyle. I love my work, but I love you more. I just want to be with you, to be the kind of wife you want and need. I'll move to Seattle gladly. And if I don't find a job or if the job doesn't last, I won't care. I'll—"

He cut off her words by covering her mouth with his own. His kiss was long and sweet and spoke more than words of his love for her. When at last he drew back, his eyes danced down at her, "You won't have to move to Seattle after all, my darling. So get that idea right out of your pretty little head."

"Why?"

"Because I'll be moving down here to be with you."

"How can you? That's impossible. Harrison Industries is—"

"Moving to Orange County," he finished. "Permanently. I own a radio station here, don't I?" He lifted her hand to his lips and planted a warm kiss on her palm. "I could have looked into buying a station in Seattle, but I saw how important it was to you to stay in Southern California. So I took a good look at my own needs and interests. Hell, I've only got a suite of offices up there. I can operate anywhere, as long as I'm near an airport. It'll take a few months to complete the move, and I'll have to do a bit more traveling than before, but I'll be here most of the time. My secretary's not speaking to me, but—'' He grinned. "At least my wife will be. On a daily basis.''

She tried to assimilate the impact of his words. "But...your family...you've lived in Seattle all your life!''

"True. High time for a change. And we'll see my family on vacations, same as yours.''

"When...did you decide all this?'' she asked, dazed. "Why didn't you tell me before?''

"I didn't contact Westler about the possibility until a week ago. By then you were out of town, and no one knew where to find you. He had another offer, so I was forced to make a decision last week. I went ahead, hoped you'd approve. Do you?''

"Do I?'' She hugged him, her heart so filled with joy she felt it might burst. "Do I ever!''

His chuckle vibrated against her chest as he lowered his mouth to hers. "Are you sure you won't mind spending every day of the rest of your life with me, Mrs. Harrison?''

"Even that won't be long enough, my love,'' she whispered before his lips claimed hers once more.

"After those thundershowers this morning, who'd expect such a gorgeous afternoon?'' Desiree smiled into the microphone. She ran her hands lovingly over the gleaming, state-of-the-art console, which Kyle had ordered the day he took possession of the station. "We've got clear blue skies all across Orange County to welcome the first day of spring. And you've got Desiree on KICK, Anaheim.''

She started a commercial break, then sat back and scribbled a To Do list for herself, one of the many efficient habits she'd picked up from Kyle in the eight months they'd been married.

1. Call travel agent. Kyle's birthday was next month, and she'd planned a surprise vacation to Tahiti. His coworkers knew all about it. She couldn't wait to see the expression on his face when she picked him up at the office and whisked him off to the airport.

2. *Go over financial statement.* The station had received its highest ratings ever in Arbitron's latest book, and they'd been able to raise their advertising rates accordingly. She'd hired an assistant manager to help with her duties, but conferred with Kyle on all major business decisions. And of course she'd kept her spot on the air. It was a hectic schedule, but the daily challenge and excitement thrilled her, and she was proud of her accomplishments.

3. *Decide on wallpaper for bedrooms.* The new house in the hills above Newport Beach was well underway. In a few months they'd be able to move in. She couldn't stop a grin as she doodled a smiling sun next to the last notation and thought about the other surprise she'd tell him tonight at dinner. *A different wallpaper for each bedroom,* she wrote. All six of them . . .

The promo ended and she switched on the mike, then flicked the lever for traffic. "It's time now to check on the traffic situation. Let's talk to our man in the skies. How ya doin' up there, Dave? Are the wet streets causing motorists any problems today?"

"No major accidents yet, Desiree." The unexpectedly deep resonant voice caught her off-guard and sent a paroxysm of delight spiraling through her. She hadn't heard his voice over the air since the day they met! Would he ever tire of finding ways to surprise her?

"I see we've got Killer Kyle filling in for Deadly Dave Dawson today," she said with a laugh. "What happened? Dave take a rain check?"

"You've got it. Thought I'd step in and take this bird up for a spin." Kyle went ahead with the traffic report, speaking smoothly, expertly, like a seasoned radio professional, giving no clue to his true identity or his lack of previous experience at this job.

"Thanks, Kyle. I hope we'll be hearing more from you," she said when he was through, unable to disguise the pride and admiration she felt for her remarkable fun-loving husband. "Before you sign off, though, I've got a news flash which might interest you. Just came in, hot over the wire.''

''I'm all ears.''

''Inside sources just announced there's going to be a new little deejay at KICK in about . . . oh, seven months or so.'' Desiree bit her lip to keep it from trembling in the silence which followed.

Finally, with a slight break in his softened deep voice, he said: ''Let me be the first to congratulate you...and your...husband. I'm sure he must be absolutely *delighted* with the news.'' He let out a sudden exultant whoop of glee. ''I've always said, what this station needs is some fresh young talent! Who wants to make a dollar bet it's twins?''

And as all the phone lines in her control booth began to flash, their joy and laughter vibrated over the airwaves.

 # Silhouette Desire

COMING NEXT MONTH

THE FIRE OF SPRING—Elizabeth Lowell
Winning the Sheridan ranch wasn't enough for vengeful Logan Garrett—he wanted Dawn Sheridan, too. Dawn was determined to teach him to love, not hate, and she'd accept nothing less.

THE SANDCASTLE MAN—Nicole Monet
Sharon wanted a child—Michael's child, but Michael was gone. Then one day Sharon met Rob Barnes, who became her fairy-tale prince... but would reality intrude on their dreams?

LOGICAL CHOICE—Amanda Lee
Analytically minded Blake Hamilton was surprised when he discovered his attraction to Diana Adams couldn't be explained away. Diana had to show him just how illogical love could be!

CONFESS TO APOLLO—Suzanne Carey
Denying her own Greek heritage, Zoe planned to quickly leave her childhood home after a business trip there. Then she met Alex Kalandris—devastatingly handsome, utterly compelling and—Greek.

SPLIT IMAGES—Naomi Horton
After TV spokeswoman Cassidy York interviewed arrogant Logan Wilde and got blackmailed, on-air, into a date with him, she was enraged. But meeting the man behind the image engendered very different emotions.

UNFINISHED RHAPSODY—Gina Caimi
When concert pianist Lauren Welles returned home to her former music teacher, Jason Caldwell, she realized she still had a lot more to learn.... But not about music.

AVAILABLE NOW:

OUT OF THIS WORLD
Janet Joyce

DESPERADO
Doreen Owens Malek

PICTURE OF LOVE
Robin Elliott

SONGBIRD
Syrie A. Astrahan

BODY AND SOUL
Jennifer Greene

IN THE PALM OF HER HAND
Dixie Browning